Carolus Deene, history-schoolmaster detective non-pareil, sums up towards the end of his latest case:

"Just once or twice in a generation there is born a murderer, a murderer by vocation, and the startling thing is that he is virtually unrecognizable. He is not a schizophrenic—his mind is far from split, on the contrary he might be called single-minded. Sometimes he begins his career quite young, sometimes he waits till he is past middle age, but most often he achieves his masterpieces when in the prime of life. In this case we had such a murderer, one who simply was not interested in personal ties, who was as cold-blooded as a fish in Arctic waters, cruel, ruthless and utterly resolute, and yet who had the faculty possessed by such murderers of appearing a normal, even an amiable person.

"This is no impulsive killing, no crime of passion, not even a murder for greed, as it turned out. Here were the actions of someone whom the psychiatrist would call stark raving mad, and whom I consider to be that *rara avis* a murderer born, a murderer by natural talent, a murderer who would stop at nothing."

DIE
ALL,
DIE
MERRILY

by
LEO BRUCE

Published in 1986 by

Academy Chicago Publishers
425 North Michigan Avenue
Chicago, IL 60611

Copyright © Leo Bruce 1961

Printed and bound in the USA

Library of Congress Cataloguing-in-Publication Data

Bruce, Leo 1903-1980.
  Die all, die merrily.

  I. Title.
PR6005.R673D5 1987   823′.912   86-32269
ISBN 0-89733-254-7
ISBN 0-89733-253-9 (pbk.)

Come, let us take a muster speedily:
Doomsday is near; die all, die merrily.

Henry IV, Part One, IV, 1.

1

Mr Gorringer leant back in his chair and brought the tips of his fingers together.

" Murder, eh? " he said, with an air of experience.

"That's what it sounds like. He described exactly how he had done it. By strangulation. Lady Drumbone thinks . . ."

" Ah! " Mr Gorringer seemed galvanized by the name. " Your mission is from Lady Drumbone, then? "

" In a sense, yes. There is certain evidence which Lady Drumbone considers should not be made public."

" She was ever a law unto herself," reflected Mr Gorringer.

He knew—and who does not?—something of the rise to fame of that remarkable woman whose personality dwarfed those of other female politicians as Buckingham Palace, by its ornate amplitude, dwarfs the dull houses in its region. Though elected a few years after Lady Astor, she soon asked funnier questions than that lady, and her baroque appearance, her monumental bust, her rich contralto voice and her discovery of curious and unpopular causes to espouse, made the credulity and *faux pas* of Mrs Braddock, Dr Summerskill and Mrs Castle seem like the mild idiosyncrasies of a trio of Sunday school teachers.

She it was who had invited Colonel Grivas to London, speaking of this ' brave Christian friend of democracy '. She who had told General Franco that it was her nightly prayer that he would recover Gibraltar. She was disappointed in Israel when its abuse of England ceased, but quickly found a friend in Colonel Nasser, with whom she was photographed during the Suez affair. She distrusted the Russians, she said, since Stalin's death, but wrote from Peking her famous article "Will China Liberate All Asia? " The details she published of torture camps manned by British sadists in Africa, Mauritius, Cyprus, Malta, Honduras, Guiana, Borneo, Tristan da Cunha, the Falkland Islands and Bermuda had won her an honoured place in the literature of flagellation and her 'demands for enquiries' into the conduct of administrators topped the record by several dozen.

She belonged to no party—any such limitation would 'shackle' her, she said, but when she rose in the Commons to ask why several thousand persons had last week been beaten to death by British troops in Zanzibar, her adherents among the pressmen rejoiced. When her rich voice promised, in view of the unsatisfactory nature of the answer, to raise the matter on the adjournment, yawns may have been suppressed but pencils flew.

"So Lady Drumbone has sent you to me," reflected Mr Gorringer complacently.

"Yes. She thought it would be wise to ask Carolus Deene to investigate. He has a reputation for being discreet."

"Just so, just so," said Mr Gorringer.

As headmaster of the Queen's School, Newminster, and so employer of Carolus Deene, who was his Senior History Master, he appreciated the correctness of the approach. Carolus Deene might have achieved a certain fame for solving mysteries which had baffled others, but he remained, and had told the headmaster that he intended to remain, a member of the school staff.

Mr Gorringer, a large and important-looking person with protuberant eyes and immense bristly ears, considered gravely. Seeing him hesitate, his visitor, a plump man of resolute appearance called Alan Bourne, continued on prepared lines.

"Lady Drumbone is aware of your Work," he said.

Mr Gorringer beamed.

"You mean my little *Wayward Mortarboard?* "[1]

Mr Bourne was puzzled.

[1] *Our Jubilee is Death* by Leo Bruce   *The Wayward Mortarboard or Thirty Years on the Slopes of Parnassus* was the title of Mr Gorringer's book of reminiscences.

"Your work here," he explained. "Lady Drumbone is interested in education."

"Ah, yes. Quite. Exactly. I see. I'm delighted. To be sure."

"She is shortly asking a number of questions in the House about the public schools which she considers degrading, demoralizing, a hotbed of vice, the canker of modern decadence, a forcing-ground for bullies and petty tyrants. In a series of articles which she will be writing at the same time for the *Daily Horror* and the *Sunday Amorial* she is prepared to omit any direct attack on this school, though she has heard its punitive system described as mediæval. Always providing you arrange this little matter for her by sending this man Deene to investigate."

There was an interruption while Mr Gorringer cleared his throat.

"I scarcely know what to say," he admitted. "It is true that neither our Governing Body nor I would seek public criticism of the kind you mention. On the other hand the holidays have just begun and I have no jurisdiction over my staff. I should like Lady Drumbone to realize that. If Deene wishes to investigate he will do so. There is little I can say to persuade him."

"Choosy, is he?"

"Since you use that curious piece of vernacular, yes, Deene is extremely choosy. I doubt whether he will undertake an investigation in which some evidence is being withheld. I can but try to prevail on him."

"Remembering that Lady Drumbone will thereupon forget this school's tradition of brutal punishments. You have, I understand, an eighteenth-century caning-block."

"It is kept as a curiosity," gasped Mr Gorringer.

"It would make a splendid illustration for Lady Drumbone's new series of articles. She will have finished with the thumb-screws of Kenya next week, then she has only a small matter of 'A Blackguardly Battalion Commander' to deal with before she starts on the schools. You see my point?"

"Indeed I . . ."

"So can we get Mr Deene at once?"

Mr Gorringer retained his dignity.

"I will send the school porter across to his house," he said, ringing a bell.

When Muggeridge the porter appeared he seemed disgruntled.

"I thought the holidays had begun," he said.

Mr Gorringer rose to this.

"They have, Muggeridge," he said airily. "That is why I want you to go round to Mr Deene's private house and ask him if he would be so good as to come across for a minute."

"It's the other side of the High Street," said Muggerridge. "Sunday afternoon, too."

"Just tell him we await him, please. At his earliest convenience."

"Well, I don't know," sighed Muggeridge and withdrew.

"You are, perhaps, related to Lady Drumbone?" suggested Mr Gorringer chattily.

"I'm her nephew. The dead man was my cousin."

"I see. She is a very remarkable woman."

"She's . . . yes, very remarkable."

"Accustomed to getting her own way, I make no doubt?"

"Never fails."

"Perhaps she should have come in person."

"Oh, she will if I can't fix it. No doubt of that."

"Dear me. Yes. We must do our utmost to prevail upon Deene."

But when Carolus came he was not alone. Rupert Priggley, his most precocious pupil, entered behind him.

"I must apologize for this," said Carolus. "Priggley has planted himself on me for the holidays again. I don't seem able to do anything about it."

After introducing Mr Bourne, the headmaster turned to Priggley.

"Why are you not with your parents?" he asked.

"Well, you know what it is, sir. Mummy daren't leave her millionaire at large for a moment and the old man's chasing something new. One of these perspiring weirdies who secretly longs for a wash and a hair-do. It's too dreary."

"So Mr Deene is to coach you?"

"That's the idea, yes, sir."

"You would have been better with Mr Hollingbourne. He has children of your own age."

"Don't I know it? They're at Frinton. Rounders on the beach."

Mr Gorringer turned to Carolus.

"You are wondering, perhaps, why I have ventured to invade your holiday-time, my dear Deene. You know me well enough, I think, to realize that I should not do so except in a matter I thought likely to be of close personal interest to you. Too jealously I guard my own privacy in the vacation not to respect that of my staff. No later than next Friday Mrs Gorringer and I set out for our annual retreat in Ostend where I stay strictly incognito at our beloved Pension Le Balmoral, from which we spend days in Bruges, I need scarcely say. No, I should not have invited you here, Deene, unless I had something that would appeal to your insatiable curiosity. That something is no less than . . . Murder! "

'Which one?" asked Carolus. "Not that case at New Cross?"

"So far from being the sordid affair you mention, of which I have been unable to avoid details in my newspaper, this concerns someone whose name is a household word . . . Lady Drumbone! "

"Got her at last, have they?"

"I should have explained to you that Mr Bourne is Lady Drumbone's nephew. His cousin has been found dead."

"Don't apologize," said Mr Bourne.

"I had no intention of it. How did your cousin die?"

"There is little doubt that he shot himself. A revolver

was beside him and he had been shot through the head from just below the chin."

"Same old routine," said Carolus. "I suppose the only fingerprints on the pistol were his?"

"It would appear so, for the police seem satisfied that it was suicide."

"But you are not?"

"Oh, yes. I'm pretty sure it was suicide. But for that there has to be a motive, surely. A man needs as much reason for killing himself as for killing anyone else. Perhaps more."

"And your cousin had none?"

"At first it seemed not. He was fit, cheerful and had what are called excellent prospects."

"Meaning that when your aunt died he would inherit?"

"Partly that. He would share the estate with me and my brother and sister and my wife and children and several other people and nobody knows quite what there may be to share. My aunt certainly gave no information. But his own prospects were good enough."

"Then where does the motive come in?"

"That's what we want you to find out. In my cousin's room was a tape-recorder, and after his death we found on it a complete recording of his last moments ending with the shot. He sat down quietly, confessed to strangling a woman, then shot himself."

"What woman?"

"We don't know. There has been nothing yet reported in the district. Interest you?"

"No," said Carolus. "It's not my line of country at all. I don't like your aunt, or what, for want of a better word, I will call her opinions."

"Besides," put in Rupert Priggley, "How corny can you get? Tape-recorders! Rich aunts and nephews!"

"Silence, Priggley," said Mr Gorringer, then turning to Carolus: "I think you underrate the possibilities, Deene. Here you have, instead of a murderer to be traced, a murder! A situation surely unique."

"It has probably been done," said Carolus flatly.

"*Ad nauseam*," added Priggley.

"I cannot claim to be versed in the by-ways of criminology," admitted the headmaster. "I can only say that the situation is refreshingly new to me. I should have thought you would find it most attractive."

"Who found the recording?"

"I did," said Mr Bourne. "I also found the body. Early this morning. I went to my cousin's flat . . ."

"Why?"

Bourne looked at him, then said slowly: "I'll explain that later. Fortunately I found the recording before I had phoned the police."

"So they haven't heard it?"

"No. That's why I've come to you. My aunt doesn't want the existence of that recording to be known."

"The first thing I should do would be to hand it over to the investigating detective."

Mr Bourne smiled.

"You could tell my aunt that."

"I could. But I shan't be meeting her. No, it's not my tea. Evidence suppressed and whatnot. Go back and tell your aunt not to be a fool."

"But, Deene," said Mr Gorringer, "if you feel so strongly . . ."

"I don't. I'm keeping clear of the thing. New Cross is more attractive than this. By the way, Mr Bourne, you say you found your cousin's body. How did you get into his home?"

Bourne did not hesitate.

"I came from his wife," he said. "She had left him. She gave me her key of the flat."

"How long since she had left him?"

"Nearly two weeks, this time. They had quarrelled before."

"You told me your cousin had no known motive for shooting himself. What about that for one?"

"You ask a lot of questions for a man who isn't interested. But I'll tell you that Richard Hoysden would never have killed himself for Pippa's sake. They quarrelled too often for that."

"You believe he killed someone?"

"Yes."

"A woman?"

"Yes."

"And shot himself in remorse?"

"Yes."

"Oh, God," said Priggley. "We'll have an Indian poison unknown to science in a minute."

Ignoring this, Carolus asked Alan Bourne what made him so sure.

"I've heard that recording," he said. "I think if you had troubled to hear it you'd be a little less sceptical about the whole thing. It may be, as your young friend says, corny, but it's also extremely unpleasant to hear the voice of a man who is lying dead in front of you. Especially when that voice is giving exact and highly unpleasant details of how he has recently strangled someone."

"Details, you say. But he does not mention her identity."

"No. Unless you can read more into it than I can."

"No doubt it's your cousin's voice?"

"Oh, none whatever. I could swear to that."

Mr Gorringer looked from one to the other.

"Why is your aunt trying to be secretive about this, Mr Bourne?"

Again Bourne gave his dry little smile.

"She has her enemies," he said.

"I won't talk about understatement," said Carolus. "Let me just say that I know what you mean."

"It's bad enough for her to have a suicide for a nephew. She might never live down a murderer."

"Yet she has known a good many, by repute, at least," reflected Carolus. "All those shocking assassins in the British army in Cyprus—remember?—who wandered from village to village slaying women and children. Don't you recall her questions in the House about that? And the 'hired thugs in British uniform' as she called them who wanted to introduce gas-chambers into Nyasaland? I remember her article well. What about the British Butchers in Bermuda? The Carnage in the Cocos Islands? She has a wide experience of bloodshed."

"But not . . ." postulated Mr Gorringer. "Not on her own doorstep, Deene. Lady Drumbone is naturally anxious not to feed the gutter-press with sensation."

"Is she? Perhaps I have misjudged her. Suppose, then, Mr Bourne, I should discover the facts of the murder. What would be your aunt's reaction to that? Would the murdered woman be yet another 'victim of military brutality'? "

"I don't know," said Bourne.

"Suppose the victim has already been found? We are rarely without an unclaimed corpse or two in the country. Suppose, moreover, that some innocent person with circumstantial evidence against him is suspected of the crime? What then? "

"I don't think my aunt has thought of that."

"Surely, Deene," said Mr Gorringer, unable to keep triumph from his voice, "this is the very crux of the thing? The most compelling reason why you should investigate? You, and you alone, might be the means of saving an innocent person from punishment, even death. Does not that drive you to take up the . . . er . . . microscope? "

There was a long silence.

"Moreover," went on Mr Gorringer persuasively, "you are, to use a colloquialism, in on the ground floor of this. Mr Bourne only discovered his cousin this morning. Too often, you have told me, you have been called in too late."

"I'll hear this recording," said Carolus at last. "But I may find it necessary to inform the police of its existence."

Mr. Bourne said he had come from Maresfield.

"I'll come over this evening. Maresfield? Isn't that one of these new towns? "

"It is, yes. My aunt is a great believer in new towns."

Again that dry smile. "Especially when they replace anti-quated and unhygienic villages."

"I see. Would ten o'clock be too late for you?"

"Not at all. My aunt never goes to bed before midnight, so you could see her after hearing the recording, if you wish."

Mr Gorringer was rummaging in a dark cupboard and finally drew forth a half-empty bottle.

"Deene, my dear fellow, Mr Bourne, a glass of sherry?"

There was no help for it.

2

THE Queen's School, Newminster is, as its pupils find themselves under the necessity rather often of explaining, a public school. A minor, a small, a lesser-known one, they concede, but still in the required category. Its buildings are old, picturesque and very unhygienic, and one of its class-rooms is a showpiece untouched from the Elizabethan age in which the school was founded.

Some years before Mr Bourne's visit to the headmaster the school had been given a little reflected fame, for its senior history master, Carolus Deene, published a successful book and did not scorn to print under his name 'Senior History Master at the Queen's School, Newminster'. The book was called *Who Killed William Rufus? And Other Mysteries of History*, and in it Mr Deene most ingeniously applied the methods of a modern detective to some of the more spectacular crimes of the past and in more than one case seemed to have found new evidence from which to draw startling conclusions.

On the Princes in the Tower he was particularly original and perceptive and he disposed of much unreliable detail in his study of the murder of Edward II. The book was highly praised and sold a number of editions.

"It doesn't, unfortunately, make Deene a good disciplinarian," said the headmaster. "His class is the noisiest rabble in the school."

Carolus Deene was forty years old. He had been a good, all-round athlete with a half-blue for boxing and a fine record in athletics. During the war he did violent things, always with a certain elegance for which he was famous. He jumped out of aeroplanes with a parachute and actually killed a couple of men with his Commando knife which, he supposed ingenuously, had been issued to him for that purpose.

He was slim, dapper, rather pale and he dressed too well for a schoolmaster. He was not a good disciplinarian as the headmaster understood the word, because he simply could not be bothered with discipline, being far too interested in his subject. If there were stupid boys who did not feel this interest and preferred to sit at the back of his class and eat revolting sweets and hold whispered discussions on county cricket, then he let them, continuing to talk to the few who listened. He was popular but considered a little odd. His dressiness and passionate interest in both history and crime were his best known characteristics in the school, though among the staff his large private income was a matter for some invidious comment.

The boys were apt to take advantage of his known interest in crime both ancient and modern. A master with a hobby-horse is easily led away from the tiresome lesson in hand into the realms of his fancy. He may or may not realize this as the end of the school period comes and he finds that he has talked for three-quarters of an hour on his favourite subject and forgotten what he was supposed to be teaching.

Carolus Deene was very well aware of his weakness but he regarded his twin interests of crime and history as almost indistinguishable. The history of men is the history of their crimes, he said. Crippen and Richard III, Nero and the latest murderer to be given headlines in newspapers were all one to him, as his pupils delightedly discovered.

17

But he could be firm as he was that evening with Priggley.

"I'm not taking you over to Maresfield," he said.

"Oh, look here, sir . . ."

"You have already given your opinion of the affair. 'Corny', you said, 'tape-recorders, rich aunts and nephews'."

"It does sound pretty *vieux jeu*, doesn't it?"

"It does."

"I suppose you regard that as a sort of challenge?"

"I'm interested."

"Only in turning it upside down. Why don't you set about proving that it wasn't Cain who murdered Abel but Adam? Or better, Eve? That would be a story."

"Because I think it was Cain. One lesson I've learnt in investigation is not to be afraid of the obvious. I shouldn't be surprised if it's useful in this case."

Priggley sighed noisily.

"I should like to hear that recording, though. Oh, come on, sir. You wouldn't want me to tell Mrs Stick what you're about, would you?"

Mrs Stick was Carolus's housekeeper, an inspired cook and a 'treasure' who so disliked his criminoligical activities that if she heard of any more she might really do what she had so often threatened and leave him.

"Blackmail will get you nowhere," said Carolus and went out to the garage.

Driving through the scented August evening he thought no more about the details given by Alan Bourne, but felt some distaste at the prospect of Maresfield ahead of him. It was, he knew, the latest and brightest of the new towns. 'It must be hell,' he thought absently, too accustomed to the ugly places in which crime seemed most at home to take it seriously. Not more than a dozen years ago a sleepy village, with a pub, a church and a shop, it now had a population of twenty-five thousand.

Twenty-five thousand what? Carolus asked the night, but like jesting Pilate did not wait for an answer. Only it seemed to him far from a jest. By the law of averages there would be nearly two thousand television aerials, one Citizens' Advice Bureau, four children's clinics, six supermarkets, twelve petrol-stations, miles of overhead wire, acres of posters, forests of pylons and four thousand similar if not identical houses with front gardens and back and . . . but this way madness lies, he thought. There had also, and not perhaps surprisingly, been suicide and possibly a murder. Whatever Maresfield was like it gave Carolus the hope, at least, of a problem such as he loved.

He asked the way of a policeman in a doorway and found that the address he had was of a large block of flats. As he was entering this he noticed that the ground floor was partly occupied by a music and wireless shop called Hoysden's. The flat he was seeking was on the first floor and Alan Bourne opened its door.

" Come in," he said.

Carolus found an air of comfort and moderate luxury. The carpets were thick and soft underfoot and some fine old furniture was noticeable. There was central heating, a grand piano and artfully shaded lights.

" This was the sitting-room. Richard was found in bed. Have a drink."

Carolus sank into a comfortable chair and lit a cigar.

" Do you want to hear the recording at once or have the details first? "

" Details, please."

" I'll do my best. It's hard to know what you will find relevant. First of all, why we live in this town. Old Drumbone, who married my aunt when he was sixty and she was in her thirties, had the manor house here and owned most of the land. It was all he had to leave her when he died just before the last war. She had been in Parliament for some years then. I scarcely knew the old man—bit of a cynic, I believe, who regarded her activities at Westminster as comedy, but seems to have been quite fond of her. There is no one left of his family that I know of. He was an only child and the baronetcy died with him.

" But she has collected round her quite a large family. You wouldn't think it, would you? People are usually surprised after she has been making a nuisance of herself in Parliament to realize that she is devoted to all of us. Her trouble is partly her extraordinary credulity, you see. Someone comes and tells her that some colonial Governor hangs his prisoners up by the feet and she screams questions at the Colonial Secretary. Some of the newspapers play up to her and she loves her publicity. But she has strong family ties, as you'll see."

" So had most of the Great Nuisances," reflected Carolus. " Goebbels, Napoleon, Jezebel, Mrs Pankhurst, Mussolini, Salome, Queen Victoria and Agrippina for a start."

Alan Bourne ignored this.

" When they decided to make a town of Maresfield my aunt was pretty shrewd. I don't know this from her but it is thought here that she ' attracted' the scheme to this locality. I gather that she did not try to hold on to every inch of farmland but instead decided to develop for herself the big house and gardens which were to become the centre of the town. She formed a company and built large blocks of flats on her own property. There are four of these, all full to bursting, and she has retained the whole top floor of one for herself.

" Now for the family. I am the oldest son of her sister, who married my father James Bourne. My parents are dead, but I have a younger sister, Olivia Romary, whose husband was killed in Burma during the war. My younger brother Keith has just had his twenty-first birthday."

" Do they live with your aunt? "

" Keith does. Olivia has a flat of her own.

" Then Richard Hoysden was the only son of my aunt's only brother. Richard was married but had no children. I have two, by the way. So there we are."

" You say that Richard's wife had left him. Where did she go? "

" London. But she came down to see me yesterday, so she was in the town at the time of Richard's death. This must be very much between ourselves, but I gathered, only gathered, mind you, that she had gone away with someone and was pretty disillusioned about it. She wanted to return to Richard."

" Then why didn't she? Why come to you? "

" You'll understand that better when you've met Pippa. She's charming but a little on her dignity always, especially in anything to do with our family. What she feared most in the world, I always thought, was a snub from one of us. She wouldn't return to Richard till I had spied out the land. She wanted me to go round and see Richard last night, and it's a pity I didn't. When I promised to go this morning she thrust her latch-key on me. I told her Richard would let me in but she said no, I might go before he was up and wild horses would not get him to the door. So that's how I came to find him."

" Have you any idea who the man might be? With whom she was in London, I mean? "

" Well, new towns like gossip as much as old ones. There has been a story about her and a man called Rothsay. Rather mysterious character. Apparently lots of money. Runs a Mercedes. He stays at the Norfolk Hotel—that's the huge thing they've made of the little Norfolk Arms, our only pub when this was a village. Yes, puts up there for a week or two every so often apparently doing nothing but phoning his bookmaker in the morning. Pippa has been seen in his car, I believe. But you can take that story for what it's worth."

" So she was in the town last evening. Was Rothsay? "

"I can't tell you that. She didn't say how she had come. I presumed by train. We're only forty-five minutes from town. Electric railway."

" Where is she now? "

" Staying with my aunt."

" Has she heard the recording? "

" Yes. They both have."

" Any comments? "

" Look here, Deene, before I try to answer that I think

21

you ought to hear the thing. It's pretty gruesome. You'll understand then how they felt."

" No. I'd rather hear the facts first."

" Well, my aunt became . . . I can only say frozen. She did not move or speak for a time. Then she said very coldly ' Who was it? ' I thought she was refusing to admit to herself that it was Richard's voice. I was glad, in a way. It would have been best for her. But no. ' Whom has he killed? ' she asked. Then Pippa grew hysterical."

" Has anyone else heard the recording? "

" Well, yes. When I put it on first I did not realize what it was. Richard's housekeeper had arrived and heard it."

" Housekeeper? "

" Well, daily help. Char. Whatever you like. A Mrs Tuck."

" What did she say? "

" She's a somewhat ferocious woman. Reputation for downrightness. I've always thought her plain rude, but I believe she is a good worker and I suppose fond of Richard and Pippa in a bad-tempered way. When it was finished she said, ' I don't believe it '. I was too staggered by the thing itself to answer her at the time but later I wanted to know what she meant. ' He may have done for himself,' she said. ' I wouldn't put that past him. But not for anyone else.' That's all I could get out of her. She's not a favourite with the family."

" Interesting, that," said Carolus. " Now tell me, what do you all do? "

" I'm a solicitor. But not my aunt's. She bought me a partnership in an old firm here when I came out of the Air Force in '46. I was born in 1920. Richard had the business downstairs, music, radio, television. It was successful and would have been more so if he'd gone all out for hire-purchase and television sets. He would rather sell a piano. He was a good violinist himself. Army during the war.

" Keith's at the artistic stage, though I don't think he can quite make up his mind where his talents lie—if he has any. He's musical. He wanted to go to RADA at one time but got over that. He tries to paint, sometimes. He writes a little—I don't know what; he doesn't tell me. But he'll probably settle down to some ordinary job when he's older. He's young for his years."

" Your sister? "

" Olivia's bone lazy. She doesn't need to do anything because there's always someone to do it for her. She's very popular."

" Thanks. Now coming to this morning."

" Yes. I did not expect Richard to be up early, but I was rather surprised when I reached here at ten and got no reply. I opened the door with the latch-key Pippa had given me and came into this room first. I noticed nothing out of place, though of course I wasn't looking for it then. I went to knock on Richard's door. It occurred to me that in spite of what she had said on the previous evening Pippa might have returned. There was no answer, naturally, and after a while I opened the door. The electric light was on."

" Sure of that? "

" Yes, though he could have turned it off quite easily. There was a reading lamp beside him with a switch in the wire. All the curtains drawn close. The room was stuffy. Richard was in a curious position on the bed, as though he had been sitting up and slumped over."

" To which side? "

" His right. He was right-handed. The pistol was on the floor beside him. There was a lot of blood half dried. I examined nothing closely. I was just going to phone the police when I saw the tape-recorder on the table beside his bed. It had run itself out.

" I knew at once that nothing should be touched but I could not resist this. I wound it back and set it in motion. It was running when I heard something behind me and turned round to see Mrs Tuck, who must have come in quietly by the front door. There was no point in stopping it then and we heard it out.

" Afterwards I decided at once what to do. I felt quite

23

confident of Mrs Tuck. I told her something to the effect that I should keep this to myself and she nodded. ‘Give it to me,’ she said, ‘I’ll put it in my shopping-bag while the coppers are here.’ So we put the tape-recorder in her large bag and I remember thinking that this had probably hidden secrets in its time but none quite as explosive.

“Having gone so far I thought I might as well have a look at the pistol. I handled it with a handkerchief. Only one shot had been fired.

“Then I called the police and I must say they were pretty quick off the mark. Within ten minutes a Detective-Sergeant and another plain-clothes man were here. Perhaps it was their first suicide since the new town was opened. They only asked me three or four questions at the time but invited me to come round later this morning and make a statement about finding the body. Meanwhile I went to my aunt’s, taking the tape-recorder which Mrs Tuck had returned to me downstairs.”

“You’ve told me their reactions. Was there anyone else in your aunt’s flat?”

“Only Keith and Pippa. My aunt has two women to work in the house but they don’t come on Sundays. Normally Wilma Day, my aunt’s secretary, would be there, but she had asked for the week-end off—most unusual for her, I gathered. Pippa had got the breakfast for the three of them. When I came in my aunt and Keith were laughing about something, but Pippa looked up rather anxiously, I thought.”

“Naturally enough, surely? She was waiting to hear what her husband had said.”

“Perhaps. Anyway, I had to break the news. It was the worst moment of all, except the actual finding of the body. You see, each of them was fond of Richard in his own way. We all were. I got it out somehow then went and took a stiff whisky-and-soda.”

“None for them?”

“My aunt’s TT. Pippa signalled ‘no’. Keith said afterwards he was feeling sick and it would have made him throw up. I felt pretty rotten myself and I knew I had to go home and tell the wife.

"My aunt asked very few questions. In fact none of us spoke much for some time. Then, when I thought they could take another shock, I told them about the recording."

Carolus sat quite still watching Alan Bourne.

"Please go on," he said. "You're being very lucid."

"I'm a solicitor," said Bourne, and again showed that swift smile which had nothing like mirth in it.

"I've told you what they said to that."

"Not what your brother said."

"Keith didn't speak, I think. He was pretty shaken. He'd always seen a lot of Richard—more than of me. They had more in common, I suppose. But when he got me alone he asked rather childishly as if I should know everything, '*Could* he have, Alan? Killed someone, I mean?'"

"What did you say to that?" asked Carolus.

"Nothing very comforting. I didn't feel like comforting anybody. 'I shouldn't have thought so', or something of the sort. You know, Deene, when a thing like this happens in a reasonably united, reasonably happy family like ours no one is very adequate to cope with it. My aunt's a strong-minded woman . . ."

"Is she?"

"Well, a determined woman, but she was as much at a loss as any of us. Quite apart from grief."

Carolus stood up.

"Now I should like to hear that recording," he said.

3

ALAN BOURNE rose.

"You'll have to come to my aunt's flat for that."

"I see. I thought it was here, since you asked me to this address."

' No. I presumed you would want to see this place. Where the shot went and so on."

" The police do that sort of thing far better than I could. Ballistics and finger-print experts. They know by now exactly where the pistol was when it was fired. Didn't anyone hear it, by the way? "

"Yes. Two lots of flat-dwellers, I understand, but they're rather vague about it. I should have thought a shot fired in a building like this would have caused a sensation."

" No," said Carolus. " It doesn't, oddly enough. I've had this situation before. People hear a bang and say afterwards they thought it was a car back-firing or something. One is lucky if they have any idea of the time."

" Both these families had their television sets on, I gather. The walls of this building are pretty solid. Mrs Tuck, who stayed here most of the day, tells me they've narrowed the time down to between ten-thirty and eleven last night, but can't be more accurate than that. So you don't want to see anything here? "

Carolus hesitated.

" What about the tape-recorder? Did it belong to Richard Hoysden? "

" It came out of stock, we suppose. He sold them in the shop, but none of us had seen one in his flat before."

" I should just like to know where you found it."

They went to the bedroom. Carolus scarcely looked at the splintered wood at the head of the double bed, but Bourne moved a small table.

" This is exactly where it was," he said. " Within reach of someone lying in bed. The pistol was there on the floor."

" You say that apparently Hoysden had been sitting up in bed? "

" That's what it looked like."

" Suicides are unaccountable, anyway," said Carolus. " There simply are no rules of likelihood. One will stand or walk even as he swallows something that means almost instantaneous death. Another, like your cousin, takes it easy. I see nothing in the position of things here inconsis-

26

tent with a carefully planned suicide. The only unusual thing about it is that instead of writing the usual note, Richard Hoysden left his last words and confession on a tape-recorder. Even that's not unprecedented."

They left the flat without more discussion and stood for a moment in the entrance hall of the block.

"Might as well go on foot," said Bourne. "It's only about seven minutes. Or I'll come in your car to show you."

They decided to walk. It was nearly eleven o'clock before they reached the building of which Lady Drumbone had reserved the top floor. They passed among the wonders of concrete and neon lighting, noting the municipal offices which had the glassy sheen of the Crystal Palace and the stark shape of something conceived by Corbusier in a cubistic nightmare. They passed two splendid super-markets, a pub which looked like a Swiss hospital and a church which looked like a prison, all arrogantly self-conscious buildings in ferro-concrete. Highest of all was Drumbone House, and when Bourne set the lift in motion it was so swift that Carolus felt as though the inside of his stomach had been left at ground level.

It was Keith Bourne, evidently, who opened the door, a rather handsome youth in a loose-lipped way, with too much brilliant gold hair.

Alan Bourne introduced them.

"I'm glad you've come," said Keith, and invited them to sit down in the entrance hall which seemed to be the main room of the house. Was it, Carolus wondered, called the lounge? Probably. It was comfortably furnished with cream-coloured armchairs on a rich green carpet. Flowers were arranged in towering tableaux which recalled Constance Spry. There were no pictures on the walls.

"My aunt will be with us in a moment," said Keith. Carolus noticed that both he and his brother spoke of 'my aunt', never using her first name. "She has someone with her at the moment."

Alan Bourne said "Who?" rather sharply.

"Only a Case," said Keith. "From Aldershot, I believe."

"Oh, God! " said Alan Bourne.

Just then a door opened and there emerged a woman as stately as an Edwardian barmaid. She was followed by a pale rather limp young man.

As they all rose, Lady Drumbone acknowledged them graciously, but before allowing Carolus to be introduced she said: "Alan, show Mr Pitchcock to the lift."

Keith was about to speak, but Lady Drumbone—and no one could do it better—discouraged him with a glance. She wanted Carolus to be formally introduced by Alan.

This, in due course, was done.

"A dreadful case! " said Lady Drumbone. It took Carolus a moment to realize that she was referring not to her nephew's suicide but to the details recently given her by the young man who had left. "A soldier, a volunteer, treated in the most bestial manner. I shall certainly raise it in the House. On the pretence that he did not wash, a number of men divested him of all his clothing in a public barrack-room. *All* his clothing. Imagine the humiliation! They then took him to the wash-rooms and most brutally scrubbed his body with hard-bristled brooms."

"*Brooms?*" Carolus could not resist asking.

"Yes. Their excuse was that they would not approach nearer till he was clean. He suffered agonies. Agonies! But the most serious aspect of the matter was revealed the following day. When it was reported to the man's commanding officer, he *laughed*! It is scarcely credible in a civilized age. As soon as I have dealt with the Belsens of the Bahamas, I shall raise this hideous affair." She turned to Carolus. "Mr Deene, I am pleased that you are with us. Let us go to the *patio*! "

The 'patio' was a roof-garden with a fountain over concealed lighting and wrought-iron furniture.

"I do not drink," announced Lady Drumbone. "But you will doubtless wish to do so. Keith, please give Mr Deene what he wants."

Carolus noticed that the offer was not made to her nephews and this caused no surprise. However, Keith brought him an intelligently measured whisky-and-soda.

" You have heard the details of Our Tragedy? "

" I have heard about your nephew's suicide. How do you account for it? "

" There is surely only one way of accounting for it. His mind was temporarily deranged."

" You think he only imagined he had killed someone? "

" That, Mr Deene, is for you to discover. It would be the most welcome solution in the circumstances, and I think a probable one. If my nephew Richard was insane enough to shoot himself, he was insane enough to believe in a wholly illusory murder."

" I see your point," said Carolus. He did. If Richard resembled his aunt he might have made himself believe anything. " I have not yet heard his recorded confession," said Carolus. " Was there anything in it to indicate *when* he had committed the murder, real or illusory? "

" Oh, yes. He says ' I have just killed her ', or something tantamount to that."

" I see. And the shot was heard about half-past ten. When was he last seen? "

Alan Bourne answered this.

" So far as we have been able to discover, when he left his shop at nearly seven. You will hear all that from his assistants."

" Yes, indeed. But supposing that we have no further information, we can allow him three hours or so for his murder. Had he a car? "

" Yes. A Rover."

" Do we know whether he used it that evening? "

" Not yet. You will probably be able to find out."

" I'm indulging in supposition," admitted Carolus. " Suppose your cousin's confession is to be accepted. Suppose when he dictated it he had ' just ', as he said, killed someone. Suppose he used his car. We have an area within a radius of say thirty miles of Maresfield in which the murder took place. Possibly a little more but probably less."

"These," said Lady Drumbone, "are as you admit suppositions. The important thing is to establish that no murder has taken place."

"That is what you want me to do?"

Lady Drumbone evaded this.

"I want you to investigate, Mr Deene. I understand that you have experience in investigation. I am naturally anxious that there shall be no scandal. I am, as you know, a public figure."

"I know that," he said. "What do you mean by scandal?'"

For a moment Lady Drumbone seemed nonplussed. She was sitting very straight but she looked down as though studying the five rings on her clasped fingers. Powerful fingers, Carolus noticed.

"I mean scandal which could be used against me," she said. "Unscrupulous people will go to any lengths to vilify if it serves their own ends and gives them publicity. A reputation may be blasted so easily."

You should know, thought Carolus, but he said only: "I'm afraid you're right. But if your nephew did murder someone?"

"If he did it was during a fit of insanity. It is most unlikely that his name would be connected with the crime."

"And if someone else were accused of it?"

Lady Drumbone rose to the occasion, both in fact and figuratively. She stood up and her tall figure was dark against the sky.

"Let justice be done!" she said loudly, if ambiguously.

"So long as that is your attitude we can go ahead. The first step will be, of course, to hand this recording to the police."

"I warned you of this," said Alan Bourne to his aunt.

"To the police!" said Lady Drumbone. "But it is precisely to avoid such a step that I am employing you. I want this matter cleared up without official intervention. My nephew's last words"—there was a dramatic ring in her voice—" are surely of concern to us, his family, not to any public body."

" Murder, or supposed murder, is very much a public concern. You yourself have frequently made it so. Need I remind you . . ."

" You need remind me of nothing, Mr Deene. I have a high sense of public responsibility. Were this a case of tyranny or suppression, such as I have frequently exposed, it would be another matter."

" Don't let's argue about it. The recording will go to the police tomorrow, or I shall report its existence."

" Please don't address me in that hectoring manner, Mr Deene! " said Lady Drumbone with dignity. But watching her Carolus knew that she was baffled and somewhat afraid.

" I don't think you need worry much," said Carolus. " The police are accustomed to hysterical confessions. They get several from quite innocent people after every crime. Unless they have on their hands an unsolved murder of a woman discovered today they'll probably put your nephew's confession down to illusions, as you do. They have murders enough without looking for them. If he did kill someone, on the other hand, they would almost certainly trace it to him, recording or no."

There was a sudden interruption from Keith.

" Richard didn't kill anyone! " he said. " He couldn't! "

" In that case there can be no reason to suppress this recording. Eight people, at least, know of it already and it can be only a question of time before the police hear that it exists."

" *Eight* people? " asked Alan Bourne.

" You yourself told Gorringer, Priggley and me. Then there are Lady Drumbone, Mrs Hoysden, Keith Bourne, Mrs Tuck and yourself. I should be surprised if you have kept it from your wife, and I would guess that your sister, Mrs Romary, has heard something of it. In a few days it will be common property, then it would look to the police as though you have been deliberately concealing it."

"There may be some small measure of truth in that," conceded Alan Bourne.

But Lady Drumbone was not prepared to give in without a struggle.

"I should be the *last* person," she announced, "to countenance the suppression of evidence. I have seen too often the evil that comes from that. The Government suppressed the evidence in that case of the three Icelandic patrol boats which were sunk by a British battleship, their crews left to drown in icebound seas lest their statements should incriminate the commander of the battleship."

"How did you know of it?" asked Carolus, fascinated.

"One rating, Mr Deene, one naval rating in all the battleship's crew had the conscience to inform me. The Governor of the Gladstone Islands suppressed the evidence when a battalion of the Ross and Cromarty Fusiliers went beserk . . ."

"You mean you disapprove of suppressing evidence, Lady Drumbone?" cut in Carolus.

"On matters of public interest, certainly. But the sanctity of family life . . ."

"Perhaps we could hear this recording now?"

"I am not accustomed to being interrupted, Mr Deene."

"Not?"

"Certainly not in my own home. But since my nephew has, foolishly, I begin to consider, brought you into this matter, you shall hear the recording. Keith!"

"I'm not going to listen to it again!" cried Keith.

"You have not been asked to listen to it. But kindly . . . er . . . play . . . insert . . . put the thing in rotation. We will return to the lounge for it. And please close the doors."

Before producing the tape-recorder, however, Keith refilled Carolus's glass. Then, leaving the tape-recorder open on a table, he walked quickly from the room.

Alan Bourne crossed to it.

"My brother is highly-strung," he explained. "He was devoted to Richard and this thing is very disturbing, as you will hear."

Carolus glanced at Lady Drumbone, once again upright in her chair, her face expressionless. The words began somewhat abruptly.

"Oh, I killed her all right. She is quite, quite dead. With a silk cord no more than a yard long I killed her and left its tassels on her shoulders like a pair of epaulettes. She never had a chance to make a sound, and if she had there was no one to hear her. But it did not matter, for I had drawn it tight before she could open her mouth. She had not time to get hold of it. Her hands came up but it was almost convulsively. A single choking cough and she could breathe no more. I had done what I meant to do."

There was a pause here, but no one spoke. When the voice resumed it was a little slower, a little weary it seemed.

"Why did I do it? Hate and love are always so damnably intermixed. I loved her, yes, but I hated her, too. I wanted to be free—as I could never be while she was alive. Yet within an hour of killing her I wanted to be under her spell again. Spell or domination? I wanted to be with her. And I'm going to be. Why I did it and why I meant to do it are different things. As I planned it all, it would give me what I wanted. But when I came to carry it out, I did not think of that. Hate and love, you see.

"When will they find her, I wonder? Tonight? Tomorrow? They may find me first and wonder. But they will find her later and understand. She will still be there. White on the green ground.

"When I think that I have just come from her, that an hour ago she was alive . . . but I won't think of that. I know what I'm going to do now.

"'Yet she must die, else she'll betray more men', I thought when I came to her. 'She's like a liar gone to burning hell'. ''Twas I that killed her'. I said that as I came away and it was true.

"Yes, I had my reasons and planned it with care. I should never be suspected, I said. I was right there, too. No one saw me. No one would ever connect me with it. It was neatly done. But I did not foresee this. Remorse? No, it isn't remorse. I don't want to go on living, though. Surely that will be understood by everyone. I don't want to live while the investigation follows her death, and someone else is suspected.

"Lucky I've got this little revolver. A souvenir. With plenty of ammunition, though I shall only need one shot. It's quite sure; no chance of bungling. Under the chin— like this—and through the brain."

There was another long pause, the same voice could be heard saying "Hell!" then the shot.

Alan Bourne rose and was making for the tape-recorder.

"No," said Carolus, who was listening intently, "let it finish."

They waited while the tape ran through but there seemed to be no other sound. It took some considerable time.

"Did you hear anything?" asked Bourne.

"No. Did you?"

"Not a sound."

"There was not a sound," said Carolus. "Not a move- ment, not a flapping blind or the mew of a cat. It does not seem natural for a flat to have been in such silence."

He looked about him.

"Let's listen here, for instance."

They were motionless. Just audible was the ticking of a large clock and from far away the noise of a car starting up in the street below. Somewhere, lower in the block, a piano was being played.

"You see? There is scarcely ever silence."

4

LADY DRUMBONE asked a question and Carolus knew what it felt like to be a Minister of the Crown when she rose.

"Have you learnt anything from that?"

"A great deal. Look, Bourne, I know it's late, but if you're going to hand that thing in tomorrow morning we must get hold of a shorthand typist tonight to take it down. Is that possible?"

"It's well past midnight."

"I know, but this is essential. It must be someone meticulously accurate and also trustworthy."

"There is only one possibility and I doubt if she will leave her home tonight. She has probably been in bed for three hours."

"Telephone?"

"Yes, but I hardly like . . ."

Lady Drumbone settled the matter.

"Better phone her, Alan, since you *have* introduced Mr Deene."

The clause seemed hardly consecutive, but it brought Bourne to a decision. He dialled a number. There was a pause of nearly two minutes before he was answered.

"Miss Tripper? Oh, this is Mr Bourne. I am sorry to trouble you at this late hour, but a matter has arisen of the utmost urgency. Yes. We need something to be taken down in shorthand from a tape-recorder. No, tomorrow would be too late, I'm afraid."

Bourne listened, then putting his hand over the mouthpiece said: "She says she's in her night attire."

"Tell her to come just as she is," said Carolus hurriedly.

"If you would be so good as to dress we would send a car for you in ten minutes. Well, a quarter of an hour, then. No, no, no, I'm at Lady Drumbone's flat. Of course she is here and will be present. My brother will come for you. Yes, yes. No, no. He will indeed. No, not on any account. But no one will *see* you. They can't be, at this time of night. I'm sure they wouldn't think anything of the sort. Not about you, Miss Tripper. No, indeed. Yes, certainly. I give you my assurance, yes. Of course not. Thank you. In fifteen minutes' time then. What? Yes, I'll tell him. No, he knows it's an urgent matter. Right. Fifteen minutes . . ."

"Put the receiver down," said Carolus, exasperated, and Bourne did so and left them for a moment presumably to send Keith with the car for Miss Tripper.

"I am still waiting to hear," said Lady Drumbone as a supplementary to her first question, "what you learned from that recording."

"A lot. I find this a most interesting case." He turned to Bourne as he re-entered. "But I am surprised at your saying your cousin had given *details*."

"Well, didn't he?"

"He gave, unwittingly I think, a great deal of information, but no details at all. He does not say whether his victim was young or old, tall or short, blonde or dark, in fact he says, directly, nothing about her at all except that he loved and hated her."

"At least from that we know she wasn't a stranger to him?"

"Do we? A man in his state of mind could believe that he loved and hated someone known only an hour. Then of the scene of the murder he does not say whether it was near or far, indoors or out . . ."

"He says ' white on the green ground '. That's a pretty strong indication."

"He gives no precise time, and as for motive he only says that he planned it with one object and carried it out with another, or words to that effect. He does not say whether he used his car or whether he left the body at the scene of the murder or moved it. He says nothing of the woman's face or dress."

"But he tells us what he used."

"That might be sheer hysterical rhetoric—' a silk cord no more than a yard long '."

"With tassels."

"Yes, but he was babbling like Othello whom he later quoted. I don't say there is no information in the thing. There is a great deal. But hardly ' details '."

"You are satisfied though, Mr Deene," said Lady Drumbone in a second supplementary, "you are satisfied that there was a murder? I hoped you might feel as we do that it was an illusion."

"That was no illusion, Lady Drumbone. There was a murder, all right."

"And you intend to discover the details?"

"I do. Now let us again go on mere supposition. If Richard was going to take someone to a place with this object . . ."

"This is very painful to me, Mr Deene."

"I'm sorry. Can either of you suggest anywhere?"

Keith passed through the room on his way to the front door, but did not hesitate. It was Lady Drumbone who answered.

"If I make a suggestion it must not be thought that I agree with your premise that Richard committed murder. But on principle I shall answer your questions as fully as possible. There *is* such a place."

Alan Bourne turned to her. "You mean the bungalow?" he said.

"Precisely. We have a bungalow on the coast some ten miles from here, Mr Deene. At a place called Marling Flats. We all use it from time to time, but nobody has been in occupation recently. It stands quite alone."

"You all have keys?"

"Oh, yes. It was like other things among us, a family concern. We are a very united family."

"May I visit it tomorrow?"

"Alan, give Mr Deene a key of Windy Hollow."

Carolus pocketed a heavy key.

"I haven't really started to draw even the first vague conclusions," he said, "but there are one or two small things I find rather puzzling at a first glance. One of them is that Richard Hoysden should have undressed, got into pyjamas and gone to bed, all, it seems, in order to shoot himself. I know the behaviour of suicides is often unaccountable, but this does seem particularly odd."

"Not if you knew Richard," said Alan Bourne. "He

loved his bed. Even in the army, he told me once, he had a reputation for getting his head down. If he wanted to read or listen to music or do a crossword in the evening he would sit up in bed. It was a family joke. We all pulled his leg about it."

" I see. So you put suicide with reading or listening to music or doing crosswords, and think he would have turned in for it? "

" He might have acted through habit or instinct."

"Yes. I suppose so. I shall have to try to trace his movements that evening and I dare say come to you both with a good many questions when I have sorted my ideas. Is Mrs Hoysden still staying here, by the way? "

Lady Drumbone answered that.

" She is. But I hope you will not wish to ask her questions. She is desperately unhappy and ill in consequence. I have given her a sleeping-tablet this evening."

" There will be no hurry for that, I think. But I shall have to ask her one or two things eventually."

They were interrupted by the entrance of Keith and Miss Tripper. Carolus rose but Alan Bourne remained seated as perhaps befitted the secretary's employer.

Miss Tripper was in her fifties and as neat as a new pin. She looked rather like a new pin, her long, narrow person rising to an inverted flower-pot hat. She seemed to be in a state of some fluster and left most of her sentences unfinished.

" I hardly know . . ." she said.

" Evening, Miss Tripper," said Alan in a businesslike manner, to put her at her ease. " Sorry to drag you out like this. Must have been very inconvenient for you."

"Oh, it's not so much the inconvenience as . . ."

" Sunday evening, too. I expect you were asleep."

" I had retired for the night, but of course . . ."

" Trouble is, there's no one else I can trust. You know my aunt. This is Mr Deene. Miss Tripper."

" How do you . . . I really don't . . . Of course, I'm quite . . ."

"Yes, yes. Now the thing is this. You will have heard of my poor cousin's suicide?"

"Yes, I was so very . . . It was a terrible . . ."

"You must know that he did not, as usual, in these cases, leave a letter to explain his action."

"Oh, dear, it does seem . . . I knew him by . . ."

"What he did leave was a tape-recording made in his last moments."

"Indeed? I hadn't heard the . . ."

"This tape-recording must be handed over to the police in the morning."

"The pol . . . Oh, my good . . ."

"Yes, it may be important evidence. But since Mr Deene is also investigating on our behalf we need a copy of the words spoken."

"A cop . . . You want me . . . It is all very bewil . . ."

"Yes. I know from long experience how accurate and fast you are."

"Oh, it's not my accur . . . I don't know whether . . . It seems an intru . . ."

"Well, try anyway, Miss Tripper. Here is the recording."

Miss Tripper produced a notebook, and once this was in her hands she became calmer though her sentences still hung in the air.

"I am quite . . . Please let it beg . . ." she said.

As the words came from the recorder Miss Tripper's pencil seemed to have life of its own. Carolus watched its course with amazement. All Miss Tripper's nervousness had left her now—she was doing the thing for which, it seemed, she had been born. Her face showed no emotion. Perhaps the sense of the words did not enter her mind.

"I shall indicate the shot with an asterisk," she announced coolly when she had finished.

But when Alan Bourne produced a portable typewriter her confusion returned.

"You want it immed . . . ? I thought tomor . . ."

"I should like it now, if you would be so good," said Carolus.

39

" Oh, very . . . I only thought . . . Lady Drum . . ."

She sat down before the portable. There was a whirr of fingers and Carolus was handed a sheet.

" I trust . . . no inacc . . ."

" There is only one," said Carolus, " but it is a serious one. You have omitted the word ' Hell '."

" Oh, reall . . . I scarce . . . Lady Drumbone's neph . . ."

" It's all right. I will insert it. Thank you very much, Miss Tripper."

" Not at. . . Delight . . ."

" You will please regard this incident as entirely between yourself and the family, Miss Tripper," said Alan Bourne. " I know I need not stress that. You have always been discretion itself."

" Thank you, Mr Bour . . . Then if I may be excu . . . I do trust every . . . So very trag . . . Good . . ."

" Good . . ." said Carolus, but at a glance from Lady Drumbone added " night! "

When Miss Tripper and Keith had left them Carolus recognized that there was only one thing to do—take leave of Lady Drumbone and drive home. Yet he had an obstinate feeling that he had left something undone. He took time over the last of his whisky as he tried to think what this could be, but at last rose to his feet.

Just as he was about to say goodnight to Lady Drumbone, a woman appeared in the archway which led to the rest of the flat. She was a lustrous creature, brilliant golden-red hair and a white dressing-gown which made her appearance more finished and smart than an evening gown would have done. Her eyes seemed to have a greenish tint but that, thought Carolus, might be the lighting. She carried herself not with the affected dignity of Lady Drumbone but as though conscious of her figure and looks.

" I heard that ghastly recording," she said accusingly.

" Pippa, this is Mr Deene. Mrs Hoysden."

She came towards Carolus impulsively.

" I've heard about you. I'm glad you've come. Richard didn't kill anyone, you know. Don't get that idea for a moment. Poor sweet, he hadn't it in him or he would have killed me."

"Did he ever try?" asked Carolus steadily.

"Try? What do you mean?"

She was staring into his eyes and Carolus felt she was asking how much he knew.

"Just that," he said, trying to make it sound as little insolent as possible.

"He . . . he wasn't a violent man. We quarrelled, yes." Then with sudden resolution—" Of course he never tried."

Lady Drumbone became very *grande dame*.

"I particularly asked you not to question Mrs Hoysden, Mr Deene. She is far from well."

"I'm sorry. Mrs Hoysden, when can I ask you a few questions?"

"What about?"

"Well, your husband. Your own movements last night. Just a few routine enquiries."

"I can't see what I have to do with it. If Richard did kill someone it wasn't me. That ought to be fairly obvious. Why me?"

"Because, Mrs Hoysden, I'm trying to get at the truth, and you strike me, if you'll permit me to say so, as someone who will tell the truth."

She turned away.

"I'd like a drink," she said.

"Darling, after that pill I gave you?"

"That pill doesn't seem to have had much effect, does it? Alan, please give me a whisky. Did you tell this man I was with you yesterday evening?"

"Yes. I did."

"I really think Lady Drumbone is right," said Carolus. "I shouldn't bother you with questions now."

"Come tomorrow," said Pippa Hoysden over her glass. "I'll tell you anything I can tomorrow."

"Thank you. Now I won't inflict myself on any of you longer. It's past one. Goodnight, Lady Drumbone. Goodnight, Mrs Hoysden."

Lady Drumbone bowed silently. Pippa stretched out her hand.

As he was on the way to the door he passed the tall french windows still open to the *patio*. They had costly curtains of oyster-coloured silk. At these he stopped, for they were held back by ornate silk cords with tassels.

He turned sharply to Lady Drumbone.

"Who was in this flat between seven o'clock and ten on Saturday evening?" he asked.

"To my knowledge, no one."

"Had Richard a key of the flat?"

"Certainly. It was his home until a year ago when he married. He kept his key."

"Were you the first to return that evening?"

"Yes. No one was here."

"But had anyone been here? Did you notice whether anything was disarranged?"

"I did not."

"How long were you alone, Lady Drumbone?"

"A short time only. Perhaps twenty minutes. Then Pippa came."

"Did you know she was coming?"

"We had no idea."

"What time did she arrive?"

"I got here at five-past-eleven," said Pippa.

"And your nephew Keith?"

"Soon after that. We all reached here within three-quarters of an hour. Now may I ask *why* all these questions, Mr Deene?"

For answer Carolus looked down at the carpet, ' the green ground' under their feet.

5

WHEN he came down to breakfast next morning in his small Queen Anne house in Newminster, Carolus found no sign of his least-favourite pupil. His housekeeper soon came in with the coffee, however, and explained Priggley's absence.

Mrs Stick was a small woman who wore old-fashioned steel-rimmed glasses and had, Carolus sometimes thought, an old-fashioned, steel-rimmed character. She was an inspired cook and a most efficient housekeeper but a somewhat exacting one, particularly when she suspected Carolus of being 'mixed up in one of those nasty murders'. She had few weaknesses but one of them was Rupert Priggley.

"The young gentleman's gone out," she said, placing on the table a highly-polished silver dish of crisply fried bacon and devilled kidneys. "You can scarcely wonder, can you? It's nearly ten o'clock."

"Holidays, Mrs Stick," said Carolus, trying to sound casual.

"Well, holidays I hope it's to be, sir, that's all I can say. You don't look well and need a nice rest. I was only saying to Stick, I said 'If he doesn't take a rest now he's got a chance, I don't know where we shall be'. I heard you come in last night. Well, this morning it was."

"Sorry if I woke you."

"It's not *that*, as well you know, sir. I'm a light sleeper and soon drop off again. It's wondering where you may have got to. I've got so's I don't know what to think. Though the young gentleman says it's nothing of *that* sort this time."

"Thank you, Mrs Stick."

"I'll make lunch a little later than usual. I've got a nice jiggot for you . . ."

"A nice *what*?"

43

"Jiggot of lamb, sir. Leg, to them that don't know better."

"Yes, I see. But I'm afraid I shan't be in to lunch. I was going to ask you to make some sandwiches."

Mrs Stick looked at him searchingly.

"If I thought . . ." she began.

"A day on the beach," explained Carolus. "Down at Marling Flats. I need some sea air. I'll take Priggley if he turns up in time."

"Well, don't forget the last time you wanted sea air down at Blessington-on-Sea.[1] All those dead bodies! "

"I trust there will be no dead bodies at Marling Flats, though of course one never knows, does one, Mrs Stick? "

"Not with you we don't, I'm afraid. Anyone would think they was working for a policeman, the way some behave theirselves."

Before Carolus had emerged from this pronominal labyrinth, Rupert Priggley came in, wearing overalls, passing Mrs Stick in the doorway.

"Just given the car a rub over," he said, having closed the door. "Well, how are we doing, sir? Murder or no murder? "

"Murder," said Carolus.

"How did you get on with the Drumbone? "

"She's a fool, but a dangerous one. I'm beginning to think that all our greatest disasters are due to fools rather than knaves. Contemporary history certainly suggests it. That woman would believe anything. If you told her that you had been kept in a dungeon under the school on bread and water and were flogged once a day with a knout, she'd ask a question in the House."

"I must try it," said Priggley. "Now, where do we start? "

"I want to swim," said Carolus. "We'll run down to a place called Marling Flats as soon as Mrs Stick has made sandwiches."

[1] *Our Jubilee is Death* by Leo Bruce

" I might just as well have gone with the Holling-bournes, after all. Unless you're what Mrs Stick calls 'up to something'."

" There *is* a bungalow there owned by Lady Drumbone."

" Goody," said Priggley, who occasionally resembled a human boy.

Driving down, Carolus gave him an account of Mares-field and the information he had gathered there, clearing his own ideas by making them articulate.

" You know, in a way, sir, Gorringer was right."

" You mean 'Mr Gorringer' or 'the Headmaster'."

" Yes, but we've started the summer holidays. Mrs Stick thinks you ought to relax and you won't do that by trying to be a schoolmaster. No, I mean he was right in what he said yesterday. 'Here you have instead of a murderer to be traced, a murder.' Gorrin . . . the headmaster called it 'unique'. It's not that, but it is a variant. Do you think we shall find a corpse at Marling Flats? "

" I don't know," said Carolus seriously.

" I'm all for something washed up on the beach, though I suppose we should miss our swim. There hasn't been a bit of real excitement since that copper took a pot at you in the Purvice affair. Plenty of fun but you need hair-breadth stuff for your reputation's sake. We can't have that in this case since it's all retrospective and the murderer's dead. But you might be lucky enough to come on some-thing rather nasty and grim, like a corpse left by the tide."

" Stop babbling, will you? "

" I suppose you want to Think." Priggley yawned. " The master brain, and all that."

Marling Flats was one of the few 'unspoilt' areas of coastland in the South, chiefly because there was nothing to spoil. Miles of uninteresting marshland were divided from the shore by a tall embankment along which was a railway line, so that the sea was invisible from the low ground behind it. Planners had graciously left this waste-land to the purpose for which it had been used for centuries, grazing. The bungalow built by Lady Drumbone was a bleak little red brick affair standing alone.

"We'll leave the car on the road by the railway," said Carolus, "and walk across."

"Walk? Why? Not stealthy approach stuff?"

"Hardly in this open country. But there's no point in advertising our visit. We may want to remain inside for some time."

"I detest walking," said Priggley. "Such an unnatural form of activity."

No one was in sight as they approached the bungalow. Even in sunshine it looked sad and ugly in its four-square slated isolation. It was not improved by a barbed-wire fence round a neglected garden in which a few windswept flowers grew among the weeds. The windows were closed and no smoke came from the chimney, but its paintwork was fresh and there were curtains in the windows, so that it combined the desolate with the genteel.

"Just right for a murder," said Priggley.

A rough carriage-way led across to the road on the landward side of the bungalow, but there was no car to be seen. Carolus looked for a bell-push, but finding none knocked on the door. There was no sound of movement from within and when he had repeated his knocking in vain he produced the key and inserted it. The door opened easily. Carolus entered and locked it behind him, removing the key.

At first it seemed that the place must be occupied. A woman's raincoat was across the back of a chair and on the table of the sitting-room a cloth had been laid for one and there was some dirty crockery. Opening a door to his left Carolus found an unmade bed with some silk pyjamas on it and the articles on the dressing-table suggested that a woman had spent time before its mirror.

There were two other bedrooms, but in these the beds appeared not to have been recently used, blankets being folded neatly on their mattresses. The kitchen was tidy, though a frying-pan which had not been cleaned was on

46

the electric stove. Beside it was a kettle and Carolus found this was still slightly warm.

"Don't know about yesterday," he said, "but it looks as though a woman slept here last night, had her breakfast and went out less than an hour ago. She's coming back, I suppose, so we may as well wait."

Having made this preliminary survey Carolus now proceeded to a more careful examination of the bungalow during which Priggley watched him with an assumed expression of cynical amusement. Carolus looked at the rubbish in the bin outside the back door, opened each of the kitchen cupboards and the refrigerator, in which was recently-opened tinned food and milk. He returned to the bedroom which had been occupied and went through the cupboards but found no suitcase or spare clothes.

"Whatever she brought her things in, she has with her," he said. "I don't think she meant to stay more than a night and she's been here two unless she's a very greedy girl or had someone with her yesterday."

"You're deduction's impeccable," said Priggley, "but I was expecting a corpse, not a girl with a good appetite. She's probably gone for more food."

"Or to a call box. Lady Drumbone has managed to get electricity connected but no telephone."

"Could be."

Carolus continued to examine every cupboard in the house, even opening a large oak chest in the sitting-room.

"Still looking for corpse? Ah, well, youth must have its fling."

"Don't light that cigarette."

Priggley asked for no explanation but returned the cigarette to its case. But a moment later he whistled—a long wolf-call.

"And don't make that repulsive noise. What's the matter with you?"

"Nothing at all. Only I've seen what you haven't. Look what's coming!"

47

From the window Carolus saw hurrying up the long track from the road a girl in her early twenties. There was time to see that she was blonde and had a good figure but no more.

" In here," Carolus said, opening the door of one of the unused bedrooms. " Settle down comfortably and don't move. I think she's going to clear out and needn't know that we've been here at all."

" What a bore you are, sir! She looked delicious."

It seemed a long time before the key was heard in the lock and the girl began to move about the bungalow. She appeared to be a conscientious person or else wanted to leave no sign of her occupation of the place. They heard the rattle of crockery, then sounds from the kitchen indicating that she was washing-up. But before she had finished this a car drew up outside and she ran to the front door.

The conversation which followed sounded rather shrill, for both the girl and the man who had arrived were excited. The doors were thin, for every word of it was plainly audible to Carolus, who remained motionless in his chair.

" Keith! *Keith!* Where *have* you been, darling? Why didn't you come? "

" I couldn't. I'll tell you. Something frightful's happened. Oh, darling! "

There was a silence during which Priggley's face showed that he at least knew the explanation for it—a long kiss.

" I waited. I didn't know what to do yesterday. I've just phoned the house—I was so desperate."

" They didn't know it was you? "

" No. I held my nose while I talked. That disguises your voice. I asked for you, but Mrs Runciman said you had gone out. What happened, Keith? "

" It's Richard."

" *Richard?* What . . ."

" He . . . he committed suicide. God, it's been frightful."

" But *Richard* . . ."

48

"Yes, I know. The last person."

"When did it happen?"

"On Saturday night, they think."

"That's why you couldn't come. Oh, Keith, it wasn't you who found him?"

"No, thank God. Alan found him on Sunday morning. Since then it's been hell. Police. Everything."

"But, darling, if he wasn't found till Sunday morning . . ."

"Why didn't I come? It wasn't that. It was Pippa. She suddenly turned up on Saturday. In a state. She wanted to make it up with Richard but wouldn't go round there till Alan had seen him. She paced about the lounge like a tigress and wouldn't go to bed. I tried everything. Offered to take her round to Richard. Offered her sleeping-pills. She simply wouldn't move. In the end I had to give up. It would have been too risky to come to you in the small hours. Had you given up hope by then, too?"

"Darling, don't be absurd. I'd *no* idea what time it was till it started getting light. You knew I hadn't a watch. You were taking it to . . ."

"Poor darling."

"Darling."

There was another significant silence. Keith continued.

"Of course I meant to come down yesterday. But I couldn't. Alan came to tell us about this frightful thing. I *couldn't* get away. Couldn't let you know, either. This is the first chance I've had."

"I suppose She's wondering where I am."

"She's not thinking of anything much but the Richard thing. You see, it's worse than just suicide."

"What do you mean?"

"He shot himself. But he didn't leave a note—he made a recording which Alan found."

"How *awful!*"

"In it he said, this is the fearful part, he said he was doing it because he had killed someone. A woman."

"Oh, Keith!"

49

" I don't believe it, do you? "

" Of course not. Not Richard."

" It was beastly to hear the thing. He gave all the details. How he had strangled her."

" But who? Who was he supposed to have strangled? "

" We don't know. He didn't say anything to indicate that. Alan's brought in a man called Deene who is supposed to be frightfully clever. He's going to try to find out."

" But he can't have done it. Richard, I mean."

" I know. Yet when you hear him describing it, it's pretty horrible."

" Poor sweet. What you've been through."

" What *you've* been through. Down here alone. Wondering what had happened to me. I'm glad you waited, though. I'm glad you didn't come back in the middle of it yesterday."

" So am I, in a way."

" We'll have to tear back. I'm only supposed to have gone out for an hour."

" What shall I tell Her? "

" Oh, anything. Your mother's ill or whatever you like. She won't ask questions. There's going to be an inquest and all that. Besides, she's scared of the publicity. If by any chance it's true, if Richard went out of his mind that evening and did kill someone, they'll take it out on her. You can imagine. I'll drop you near the station and you can walk round."

" I'm to know nothing about it? "

" Not unless it's in the papers this morning. I never thought to look."

" I must finish cleaning up here. Oh, Keith, what a *ghastly* thing to happen! "

There were sounds of hurried movements in the kitchen.

" Don't bother too much. Next time we come down nothing will be noticed."

" I must put the bed-clothes back as they were. Help me fold them."

In another five minutes they had left the house. Carolus

heard the key in the lock, but motioned to Priggley to remain in his chair while the car was started and driven away.

"A nice little idyll, I *must* say," was Priggley's comment as he lit a cigarette. "Who were the *dramatis personæ*?"

"He is Keith Bourne. Younger brother to the nephew of Drumbone who has dragged me in. She, I think it's safe to assume, is Wilma Day, Drumbone's secretary. I was waiting for him to use her name but he didn't."

"He didn't use any name. Only that sickening 'darling', 'darling' all the time."

"Jealous?"

"You wouldn't let me see her properly. She looked pretty good in the distance. Now what?"

"Now we eat our sandwiches. There's some beer in the kitchen."

They settled down in the sitting-room and for a time were content to eat, for one of Mrs Stick's accomplishments was sandwich-making.

"It's disappointing, in a way," said Priggley. "We come down to find a corpse and all we get is a rather sugary love-affair."

"Don't be facetious," said Carolus. "Murder is not funny."

"But since you're convinced that there has been a murder it may just as well be you who finds the body."

"I suppose so."

They were as scrupulous as the lovers had been in clearing away evidence of their visit, leaving only two empty beer-bottles to show someone had been in the bungalow.

"I don't like this place," said Priggley, looking about him. "There's something rather sinister about it."

Carolus looked up.

"What makes you say that?"

"Oh, I don't know. Expensive furniture ordered as a lot. That hideous green carpet. Can you imagine people coming down here for a week-end and enjoying themselves?"

51

" I can't imagine much fun where the Drumbone is, certainly. Let's get away."

" Maresfield? "

" Yes. I have to see the woman who was ' in a state ' on Saturday before her husband's death had been discovered, but who seemed perfectly calm last night. Let's go."

6

ON reaching Maresfield Carolus disembarrassed himself of Priggley.

" Go to a cinema or find someone in a pub who will listen to your sparkling chatter," he said. " I want to see Mrs Hoysden alone."

" Like that, is it? All right. What time shall I meet you? "

" Half-past ten outside that curious town-hall. If I'm a little late, hang on. I'm going to take Mrs Hoysden out to dinner."

" God! Where? "

" There's a restaurant a few miles away which is sup-posed to be good."

" What kind of good? Roast beef of old England or phony French? "

" I don't know. But at least it will enable me to get her out of that flat of Drumbone's."

He telephoned and asked for Mrs Hoysden, then explained quite frankly that he did not want to come to the flat just yet, and suggested that she should dine with him, not in the town but at a restaurant some miles away. She seemed quite calm and agreed at once. Her readiness for a tête-à-tête might mean that she had nothing to con-ceal or it might mean, Carolus thought, that she wanted to give the impression that she had nothing. He agreed to call for her at seven o'clock.

"Get the porter to phone up when you arrive," she said; "it will save you coming to the flat at all."

She came out to the car looking splendid. She wore black but no one would have supposed it was mourning. Yes, noted Carolus, the eyes were green—it had not been the effect of light yesterday. She seemed curiously serene for a woman involved in a tragedy.

"I don't know what you're going to ask me," she said as Carolus drove away, "but I'll try to be as frank as a woman can when she discusses her husband."

"Thank you. I'll leave it to you to tell me what you want. Naturally, anything about Richard Hoysden is helpful, especially coming from someone who is not by birth a member of his family."

They found the Escargot de Bourgogne a Victorian villa standing back from the road with a restaurant beside it, built chiefly of metal-framed glass. A great many rose-shaded lights were visible in this and the proprietor lay in wait for them in the doorway, a large bald Londoner with a manner of speech found only in old numbers of *Punch* as the language of English-speaking Frenchmen.

"Would madame wish to have a table near ze centre?" he enquired. "Or perhaps she would prefair *au coin*?"

"This will do," said Pippa.

A vast menu was produced.

"Oh, I just want something . . ."

"We 'ave only ze table d'hôtel, madame." Then, coming to business. "Two pounds. You 'ave *cantaloup glacé à la Duc de Rochefoucauld* . . ."

"Did he like melon?" asked Carolus.

"Zat is ze name, sair. Or *Saumon Fumé Monseigneur*."

Tinned or frozen, thought Carolus.

"Or *Crème de Tomates Marquis de Polignac*."

Heinz, thought Carolus, but perhaps the best bet.

"Then," continued the proprietor triumphantly, "we 'ave *Morue Grillée Saint-Germain*, or *Vol-au-Vent de Volaille à la Bénédictine*, or *Omelette aux Champignons* . . ."

It went on inexorably to the inevitable *Glace Vanille*, a

totally uninteresting menu with pretentious trappings. The wine list was worse.

At last, however, they were alone.

"The awful thing about Richard," said Pippa, "was that he would have *liked* this. In certain ways he was as credulous as his aunt. *A la Duc de Rochefoucauld* would have got him. He had taste only in music. He was in some things a very conventional man, which makes this all the more incredible.

"I met him less than two years ago in London. We got on at once and saw a good deal of each other before he told me he was Lady Drumbone's nephew. I thought that was a pretty dreadful thing to be and said so, a remark that didn't go at all well. None of the family have much sense of humour, you know. He wasn't a fool but he was fond of Drumbone. 'Whatever may be said about my aunt,' he told me rather stiffly in reproach for what I had said, 'she is absolutely sincere. No one can doubt that, even if she is a little misguided sometimes.' 'Misguided?' I said, 'she's led up the garden. She can't *really* believe all the stories she trots out.' But he wouldn't have it. There was a lot of truth in what she said, he would have me know. He was quite upset and we didn't see each other for a week after that.

"I ought to have seen the red light. I ought never to have met him again. But I was fond of him then and couldn't believe the old girl dominated him like that. Then I agreed to come down to Maresfield and meet her."

Pippa was interrupted by the waiter, but Carolus did not speak. He was listening intently.

"What is nothing short of terrifying about the Drumbone," continued Pippa, "is that she does believe these stories. Richard was quite right; the woman is sincere. Of course, once she has that reputation she can be led on by any charlatan or any malcontent. She really goes to places and listens to people telling her how they have seen torture camps and what not. She has no discrimination at all. But she is also very fond of her family. She's a sort of baulked matriarch. Alan, Richard, Keith and Olivia—you haven't met Olivia yet—and, I suppose Alan's wife Anita and me and her secretary Wilma Day. She wants to run all our lives for us. It's genuine enough and not altogether selfish.

" But I still did not realize it when I agreed to marry Richard. I knew I should be one of the family, as it were, but I did not know how much.

" In Richard's case it was strange because he wasn't brought up by the Drumbone as Keith was. Richard was thirty-two when I married him a year ago and his mother had been dead only four years. Yet he was the most under the old girl's thumb of any of them. No, that's not right. They weren't under her thumb exactly but they—made her the centre of things, if you know what I mean. Richard particularly."

" I can guess, I think."

" He was so good-natured. He'd do anything for anyone. If old Drumbone wanted to be treated like a Grand Duchess she had to have it. He would no more refuse her that than the loan of his car. But I must say it began to bore me. I didn't want to be a member of any family. I'd had enough of that with my own. So I began to . . . rebel. I can't find the words I want this evening. This *vol-au-vent's* hell, isn't it? "

" Hell," agreed Carolus. " Never mind the exact words. I understand your meaning perfectly."

" I mean I began to behave badly. Do things on my own. Show them all that I was not one of them. I loved Richard but I hated his . . . *conformity*. Running round to see poor Olivia. She'd been ' poor Olivia ' ever since her husband was killed and she traded on it. The perpetual widow. Richard visited her as though he was visiting the sick, and she's a strapping girl who ought to have married again. Keith I didn't mind so much, though he was always coming to Richard for advice, or with schemes for something he wanted to write or paint or compose. But he at least had manners, not like that dreary son of Alan's. He's eighteen, spotty and self-opinionated. When the grammar school opened here Alan took him away from Lancing and sent him to the local school to 'help start it'. That was Drumbone's idea, I think. Wait till you see the cocky young brute. He slopes about in his school cap with a pair of shaded glasses which looks absurd to start with. Richard talked music with him and gave him gramophone records. I wanted to clock him.

"Then with Alan himself he was far too generous. Alan's all right, but he has never quite grown up. And I can't stand Anita, who is a common little bitch trying to imitate her husband's aunt. Richard wanted me to be friends with her. Can you wonder that I got out of line?"

"Like most people," smiled Carolus, "I've had my experience of families."

"They're misery. Always. I can't eat this chicken, I'm afraid. I think it's a pterodactyl."

"I'm not making much progress with the *Queue de Boeuf Florentine.*"

"Taste nasty?"

"No. It doesn't taste at all. Been in the tin too long. Let's have some coffee and brandy."

"Anyhow brandy."

"Please go on with what you were saying about families."

"It was a pity, really, because Richard and I might have made a success of marriage if we'd been left to ourselves. But we never were. However, I'm not going to make excuses. Ten day ago I went off with a man called Sandy Rothsay."

There was a long silence. Pippa drank most of her brandy.

"I don't know how much you want to hear about that," she said.

"I don't know how much is relevant."

She gave him a rather sad smile.

"Nor do I, quite. Perhaps I'll just say it was a failure. You'd better meet him for yourself if you want to know

56

why. He blamed Lady Drumbone, rather unfairly, I think. 'While that old bitch is there,' Sandy said, 'she'll never let you escape her damned family.' He was very bitter about it."

"Did Richard know you were with him?"

"Yes. I wrote and told him. But I didn't tell him why I'd left him. It was not so clear to me then."

"You don't know how Richard took it?"

"Yes. Alan has told me. It's most unflattering. He was quite calm about it. Almost his only comment to Alan was 'Oh, she'll come back'. What could be more maddening? Because, of course, I did come back. At least, I meant to."

"Before you come to that, to Saturday evening, I mean, will you tell me a little about Richard. Was he never violent? In *any* way?"

"Never. The most easy-going person with everyone. That's what annoyed me, I think. I simply could not make him angry. He was so *forgiving*, you know—not in a self-righteous way, but by nature. That's what makes that damned tape-recording so impossible to believe. You're probably tired of hearing everyone say Richard couldn't have done it."

"Yet there it is."

"The only possible explanation is some sort of schizophrenia. I never saw any sign of it, though. Could it suddenly take possession of someone?"

"I don't know. I'm not a pyschiatrist."

"Madness, anyway. The voice was Richard's all right, but it was not Richard speaking. Not Richard as I or anyone else knew him."

"We'll come to the recording presently. I only wanted to know if a violent, or hysterical, or vengeful side to his character had ever shown itself, even for a moment."

"Never."

Carolus ordered two more brandies.

"When did you decide to return?" he asked.

"You'll think me idiotic, but I suppose it was as soon

as I had gone away. Even before, perhaps. I mean, some part of me knew all along that it was crazy and didn't mean anything and that I would come back. But in a practical sense, not till Saturday morning."

"When did you arrive in Maresfield?"

"About nine p.m., I imagine."

"Did you drive down?"

"Yes. I suppose this will sound rather preposterous, too. I asked Sandy to drive me down. Or rather, to let me drive his car down with him in it. I loved driving that Mercedes of his. Perhaps that's why I went away with him."

"Are you a good driver?"

"Mm. Mechanic, too. I'm tough, didn't you know?"

"And he did?"

"Yes. Why not, when you come to think of it? He'd taken me away."

"It's a little hard to visualize. What about your luggage, for instance?"

"We took that to the Norfolk, where he often stays, and left it there. I hadn't got much. I suppose that's evidence that sub-consciously anyway I meant to return. Sandy was going straight back to London, he said. I phoned Alan."

"You didn't go to his home?"

"Heavens, no. With Anita there and Charles? Charles is the overgrown schoolboy son. No, I asked Alan to come round to the Norfolk. I wanted him to see Richard before I did. I'm a bit of a coward, perhaps, but I really couldn't arrive on the doorstep and take the risk of being politely turned away. (Oh, yes, Richard would have been polite about it.) Alan understood but said he couldn't go that night. They had some friends to dinner and he had escaped for half an hour but had to go back. He promised me faithfully to go first thing in the morning."

"Did you give him your latch-key?"

Watching her carefully Carolus saw her hesitate, then speak sharply, almost defiantly.

"Yes. What about it?"

"It seems an odd thing to do. After all Richard would let him in."

"You didn't know Richard. I doubt if a fire alarm would have got him out of bed on a Sunday morning. Alan was going early so I insisted on his taking the key to be sure of getting in. I don't see anything odd about it."

"Did you stay at the Norfolk?"

"Good gracious no. I went round to Lady Drumbone's. That would have been the end, if she heard I had stayed in a hotel in the town. I told her I wanted to go back to Richard. She was very sensible about it and thought I had done wisely to send Alan first. Because he was one of the family, I suppose."

"What time did you reach her flat?"

"After Alan left me at the Norfolk I had a couple of drinks. They close at half-past ten and I asked them to phone for a taxi. I must have reached Lady Drumbone's just after eleven."

"Did you find her alone?"

"Yes. Keith came in soon afterwards and seemed flabbergasted to find me there. But he was very sweet and tried to be helpful—offered to drive me round to Richard's and what not. I was in a bit of a state, you know. I stayed up talking to him after Drumbone had gone to bed until quite late. I think he was longing to get to bed."

Carolus smiled but said nothing.

"At last I turned in. It must have been about one o'clock. Rather unexpectedly slept like a top. Then, in the morning, Alan arrived with the news. You can see I've had a hell of a time, can't you? Alan told it as gently as he could, but when I heard that damned tape-recording it pretty well broke me. I still can't understand it."

"If you feel up to it let's consider that tape-recording for a moment. Lady Drumbone's theory is that Richard had the illusion he had killed someone."

"Richard wasn't the sort of man to have illusions."

"All right, but this wasn't the Richard you knew, it was

59

the Richard who made that confession. Now *if* it was an illusion, do you think he could have supposed it was you he had killed? 'I loved her, yes, but I hated her, too.' Could that apply to you? "

Pippa considered deeply.

" I honestly don't think so. I'm sure he never hated me. Perhaps he didn't love me much, either. We got on fairly well when I behaved myself, but these violent emotions don't seem to fit."

" I see. Can you think of anyone he might have been thinking of? "

" No. It's Richard's own character that makes the words seem nonsense. He was a most temperate man."

" But—you won't mind my asking this?—was there anyone else who aroused even his temperate emotions? "

" No one I knew of. Unless he met someone in those last ten days. It doesn't seem likely."

" Then you don't think he was just imagining it? You think he really did go out of his mind and killed someone? "

" I don't know. How can you guess what someone whom you have always known as sane would do when he is insane? "

" You can't. I shouldn't have asked you that. What about that sudden ' Hell! ' at the end? It seems rather out of keeping, doesn't it? "

" It's strange you should say that. To me it's the only thing *in* keeping. The one word that sounds like Richard. He never really swore, not even ' damn '. Hell! was about as far as he went, but he used it often. A characteristic little exclamation of his. If I hadn't known from the voice all through that it was Richard, I should have known from that."

" Thank you very much, Mrs Hoysden. You've been very explicit and patient. I must apologize for this repulsive meal, too."

Pippa smiled, but not very cheerfully.

" I suppose I seem callous," she said. " I'm not really."

She rose. Carolus, who had paid a monstrous bill, followed her out to the car.

" I hope you clear up this beastly thing," she said.

" I will," promised Carolus. " You may have helped me more than you realize."

7

Mrs Stick was waiting up for them. Carolus knew at once from her manner that something had taken place during the day which had disturbed the little woman. She followed Carolus to his sitting-room.

" Your whisky's out," she said unnecessarily, "and a bottle of light ale for the young gentleman."

" Thank you, Mrs Stick," said Carolus airily.

" Mr Gorringer's been here," said Mrs Stick in a low, fateful voice.

" Oh? What did he want? "

" It wasn't so much what he wanted as what he told me. I must say I never thought you'd demean yourself, sir, if you'll pardon the expression, not to telling me one thing when it was a case of another. So it *may* be a relative of Lady Drumbone's, and Mr Gorringer quite willing for you to get mixed up in it, that doesn't mean you was going swimming as you said, when all the while there's this man been strangling women and done for himself and you starting all over again, though you've told me I don't know how many times it would be the last."

" Ah, well," said Carolus, pouring out a whisky-and-soda.

" I'm beginning to think Mr Gorringer's as bad as any of them, upon my word I am. It was him used to want you to have nothing to do with murders and that, and now he seems to go out of his way to find them for you. I was only saying to Stick, we can't go on like this, I said, not if Mr

Gorringer's going to start. Well, can we? Then there was the dinner. You never told me you wasn't going to be in and I had some lovely ritz der voo braisay for you. Though the jiggot's still in the house. It will mean something's got to be wasted, and I do hate waste."

"I am sorry about that, Mrs Stick. I should have phoned you. Though I've been punished, I assure you, by the dinner I've had. The sweetbreads will be all right to-morrow, won't they?"

"Not the same, they won't. Keeping the young gentle-man up till all hours, too. It's not right, really it isn't. Still, I suppose it's no good me saying anything. I might as well save my breath. Mr Gorringer's coming round in the morning, he says."

"What for?"

"He's off to Belgium, he told me, and he wants to see you before he goes."

Carolus had scarcely finished breakfast next morning when the headmaster appeared. He was evidently anticipating the pleasures of Ostend (with days spent in Bruges) by wearing his holiday attire, flannel trousers, an alpaca jacket and a Panama hat. He seemed in high spirits, even after seeing Priggley smoke a cigarette.

"Ah, Deene. Ah, Priggley," he greeted them. "A brief visit before I take flight for a sunnier clime. You are already in the toils of detection, I gather. You will be pleased to hear that when I called yesterday I was able somewhat to mollify your excellent housekeeper by telling her that in this case it is at my behest that you have re-entered the lists."

"So she says. She had no idea till then that there *was* a case."

"All is well now, however. Not for nothing have I a reputation for wearing *le gant glacé*. Have you made much progress?"

"Some, yes. It's a curious case."

"And Lady Drumbone?"

"What about her?"

"She is pleased, doubtless, with your intervention?"

"Not very. I told them to hand that recording to the police."

"Was that necessary, Deene? Surely the words spoken in that recording might be construed as a moment's aberration? In Lady Drumbone's position as one of the most . . . *positive* of our politicians . . ."

"Whatever she is, she can't afford to suppress evidence. When do you leave?"

"Friday. Or as Mrs Gorringer more wittily puts it, to-morrow and tomorrow and tomorrow. On Saturday morning we shall be enjoying our *petit déjeuner* at Le Balmoral, the cares of state for some time left behind. I came this morning but to remind you that although I am willing, nay anxious, that you should render Lady Drumbone every assistance in your power, yet I should be highly displeased by a public connection of your name with the case or the remotest reference to the school. I am sure you appreciate that. As for Priggley . . ." The headmaster's prominent eyes took in his precocious pupil, who was almost supine in an armchair. "I trust you have some suitable holiday task to keep him occupied? Splendid. Splendid. Then I will wish you, my dear Deene, a happy solution to your little problem and a pleasant holiday."

"Thank you, headmaster."

"Ah, I was forgetting to tell you, Mrs Gorringer made one of her wittier sallies. 'I hope Deene doesn't find that Maresfield turns out to be a mare's nest!' she said. I must say I laughed heartily."

"I'll bet you did," said Carolus.

When Mr Gorringer had taken his departure Carolus looked at his watch.

"I want to see something of Richard Hoysden's shop, this morning," he said. "I should like to know what his staff thought of him. Coming?"

"Will it be open?"

"Yes. If I know anything of small towns, new or old, it will be busy."

He was right. This was the first morning on which 'Hoysden's' had opened since the tragedy, and several people remembered gramophone records they wished to buy or even hire-purchase instalments to pay. But it was not difficult to pick out the assistant in charge from the rest of the staff, for the formal black jacket and striped trousers of Mr Toffin, his air of importance and his hands clasped behind his back as he surveyed the scene, identified him at once. He had evidently been warned of Carolus's coming visit.

"Perhaps you would like to come into the office?" he whispered, and led Carolus to a glass-partitioned compartment at the back of the shop.

"Terrible thing," he commented austerely.

"How does it leave matters here?" was Carolus's first unexpected question.

"The business, you mean? Oh, we haven't thought of that yet."

"I suppose he left a will?"

"That is outside my sphere, Mr Deene. The family will be able to inform you, no doubt."

"What about your job?"

"I really haven't considered it. It has been a most severe shock. But I have always understood that in case of any accident or illness which Mr Hoysden might suffer, it would fall to me to carry on."

"I see. So you're likely to be manager?"

"I imagine, though I've scarcely given a thought to the matter, that a limited company will be formed in which the majority of shares will appertain to Mr Hoysden's widow. But in view of my service with Mr Hoysden—I have been here since the shop was opened—I have no doubt that I shall be asked to assume the duties of managing director. In that case I should be inclined to develop the hire-purchase side of the business and perhaps engage one or two canvassers of good presence and address. Not that such things have occupied my thoughts for a moment."

"No. No. Still it's an ill wind that blows no one any good. Tell me about Richard Hoysden."

"My late employer," said Mr Toffin primly, "might be described as a perfect gentleman . . ."

Carolus looked straight into the watery grey eyes.

"Now tell me the truth," he said.

Mr Toffin stirred uneasily.

"He was no business man," he replied at last.

"No?"

"If it had not been for my untiring efforts, Mr Deene, this business would have lost money instead of showing the very handsome profit it does. That is why I am ready and equipped to step into the breach. Not that I would wish to push myself forward."

"Richard Hoysden was too good-natured?"

"You can call it good-natured if you like. To my mind his attitude was culpably lax, even foolish. That nephew of his, for instance . . ."

"Charles Bourne?"

"Yes. If I told Mr Hoysden once I told him a thousand times not to give him credit. Throwing money away, that's what it was. Records, sheet music, he was after a saxophone . . ."

"Really?"

"I assure you. On that very last morning he got Mr Hoysden to himself for a few minutes and I saw him going hammer and tongs after something. I tried to interrupt but they stopped talking when I approached with some papers to sign. Naturally, if things are adjusted here as I have every right . . . reason to hope, I shall send that young man's account to his father. He was impolite the other day to Miss Hipps."

"Who is Miss Hipps?"

"She is my . . . our . . . the second assistant here."

"You were saying that Mr Hoysden was unbusinesslike."

"Worse than that, I'm afraid. More than once we have not been able to account for discrepancies in the petty cash until Mr Hoysden admitted that he had helped himself to the firm's money."

" But it was his, surely? "

" I see you have no commercial training, Mr Deene. The business belonged to Mr Hoysden, but that could not possibly justify him in pocketing funds right, left and centre without a by-your-leave or a word of explanation. It caused great confusion and might have led to suspicion falling on some innocent party if I had not confidence in my . . . our . . . the staff."

" You had differences of opinion with Richard Hoysden, then? "

" I should not like to voice a word of criticism now, but he could be most exasperating. He never seemed to appreciate what his staff did for the business. Even Miss Hipps, who was always the soul of devotion, could not help remarking on that."

" Had you noticed any change in Mr Hoysden recently? "

" That is a difficult question. Mr Hoysden did not discuss his private affairs with his staff but it was, of course, known to us that his wife had left him."

" Why 'of course'? She might have gone away to stay with friends for a few days."

" It is clear that you have no experience of a staff of young ladies, Mr Deene. In business like this . . ."

" Yes. I can guess. Go on."

" Miss Hipps herself could not help passing the remark to me that she was not surprised. Mrs Hoysden did not inspire much respect. Her association with a guest at the Norfolk Hotel had been noticed, and when finally she showed her true colours, there was a great deal of sympathy for Mr Hoysden. But since you ask, it was generally felt that Mr Hoysden showed indifference at her departure, if not relief. Miss Hipps went so far as to say it was a good thing."

" Now coming to Saturday. Still no change in Hoysden's manner or behaviour? "

" No marked change, no. I thought him perhaps a trifle absent-minded, but that was not unusual."

" Did any of the staff notice anything? "

" I think not. But it chanced that I had Mr Hoysden's permission to leave early that day."

" At what time? "

" We close at seven on Saturdays. I left at five. A meeting of the Amateur Dramatic Society which I could not possibly miss."

" So you have an amateur dramatic society. Is it successful? "

" I am glad to say that in the last year I . . . we have achieved no little success. We have a number of enthusiasts —Miss Hipps is our leading lady."

" Any of Lady Drumbone's family join? "

Mr Toffin looked severe.

" None of them acted. Doubtless they considered themselves above our efforts. I approached Mr Hoysden more than once for he had an unusually rich and dramatic speaking voice, I considered, and had been asked to read the Lessons at church. But no. ' I'm too lazy, Toffin,' he said with a smile. As for Mr Keith Bourne with his high-falutin' ideas, he would not have stooped to *amateur* dramatics."

" Had you any recruits in any way connected with Richard Hoysden? "

" Yes. One of our best character actors, when he could be persuaded to take an interest, was the porter in this block of flats. Slugley, his name is. Excellent in the rôle of the butler—a rôle which is frequent in modern drama, I notice. Also a Mrs Nodges who lives above Mr Hoysden's flat. A cast in herself, I assure you! "

" I should think so."

" I'm not saying that we could not have had a representative of the family. Mr Alan Bourne subscribed, though he took no active part. He was anxious that his son should be given important rôles. ' Oh, no,' I said, for the young man was quite without talent in my opinion, though he had a high opinion of himself and once told Miss Hipps that he believed he could write a play. But I was against that. However, I was telling you that I left the shop early to attend a meeting of the Society."

67

" So who was in charge, under Mr Hoysden? "

" Oh, Miss Hipps, of course. My second in command here."

" Perhaps I could see her for a moment? "

" I'll call her at once."

" Just one moment, Mr Toffin. Is there nothing you can tell me which may throw light on this thing? "

" I fear not. I was not on intimate terms with Mr Hoysden. He did not confide in me. He never once, for instance, invited me to his flat though it was in this very block. I can suggest nothing to account for his suicide."

Mr Toffin sounded somewhat huffy as though he resented Richard Hoysden killing himself without prior consultation with his senior assistant.

" I was thinking of more concrete things. The tape-recorder, for instance."

" Oh, that. It came out of stock. It must have been removed that evening. It was certainly in its place when I left at five."

" Thank you, Mr Toffin. Now if I might see Miss Hipps? "

" We cannot both be absent from the shop. I will ask her to come in to you." Mr Toffin peered through the glass partition and frowned. " Did that young man come in with you? " he asked. " I ask you to observe! "

Carolus observed. He might have guessed. While the customers looked on in wonder, Priggley was apparently performing, with one of the ' young ladies ', some of the more violent and exhibitionistic steps of a dance to the loud music of a record-player.

" Disgraceful! " said Mr Toffin. " In the circumstances, scandalous! "

He dashed out and Carolus heard him shout " Miss Gibbons! Really, Miss Gibbons! " The music ceased. " You forget yourself! "

" It's not her fault," said Priggley at once.

" We won't discuss that, thank you."

" I dragged her out," said Priggley.

" Perhaps you also instructed her to twist herself into a position from which she could look between her own legs? "

Carolus interrupted.

" Go and wait for me at the Norfolk," he told Priggley curtly, and order was slowly restored.

Miss Hipps came to the office. She was in her thirties, one of those rotund, downy women on whose persons one looks in vain for a line, an angle, a point, finding only curves and protuberances. Her ears were oval, her eyes rounded and blue like the eggs of wild birds, even her fingers seemed to curl and her nose was as pudgy as a piece of dough. As though to attune with these undulations and globes she wore large orbicular beads, obtuse shoes and a silk jumper with a rounded top showing the fleshy curves of her shoulders and her bulbous elbows. Her manner was arch but confident. She spoke before Carolus could.

" I hear you want to ask me about poor Mr Hoysden. I'm afraid there is not a great deal I can tell you, though I *can* say that if anyone here in the shop knew him it was me."

" You . . ."

" Not that there was anything *in* it; we were just good friends, but I *must* say that whenever he wanted anything he always turned to me first. ' If you can't do it, Louise,' he used to say—my name's Louise—' I'm sure no one else can.' ' It's a pleasure, Mr Hoysden,' I would tell him, for he always remained ' Mr Hoysden ' to me even when he asked me to come in the car with him, on business needless to say. He was, after all, my employer and I'm sure I shouldn't have wished it any other way."

" What other way? " Carolus could not resist asking.

Miss Hipps seemed daunted for a moment but soon saw her escape route.

" *Any* other way," she said. " Though I *couldn't* help thinking that the woman he married—I mean, anyone could see they weren't suited, to say the least of it. It's not for me to pass any criticism, but when I actually saw her with my own eyes going into the Norfolk with a man . . ."

" Perhaps she wanted a drink."

" I dare say she did and it wouldn't be the first time, because the young lady who works at Middleton's the wine merchants told me his orders had doubled since they were married."

" There were two of them, surely? "

" But Mr Hoysden didn't drink much and I always thought you could see it in her face. Not that she was anything but polite to me, though I *had* to notice that she didn't get on much with the family in spite of her being related to a lord, or so she is supposed to have told someone."

" Did you notice much change in Mr Hoysden after his marriage? "

" Well, it was never quite the same."

" What wasn't? "

" Well, him. He'd always seemed to count on me somehow. Little things, you know, but I couldn't help noticing them. I think he realized it himself, for he said to me one day, ' What do you do with yourself, nowadays, Louise? I never seem to see you out of business hours.' Not that he'd seen much of me before, but it does *show*, doesn't it? "

" Yes," said Carolus, wondering in what he was assenting. " I understand that on Saturday Mr Toffin had to leave early? "

" Well, it was very rare because Mr Toffin is a great one for time and everything has to be on the dot, but he'd got a meeting of our dramatic society which he could not miss, so he asked Mr Hoysden if he minded. Of course Mr Hoysden said he could go, which was just like him, easygoing you see, not thinking of us here on a Saturday evening short-handed. Then he told me, ' It's all right, Louise. I shall be here till closing-time,' so I said ' Thank you, Mr Hoysden. I can manage if you want to go off anywhere.' "

" Was he here till closing-time? "

" Yes, he was. But just after Mr Toffin left he had a phone call."

" Not unusual, surely? "

" Well, it was for him. I could see him sitting here at the phone, it must have been for quite ten minutes, and I thought ' It's a lot of good your staying to help if you're going to sit there at the phone all the time.' I *did* wonder if it might be *her* ringing him up."

" Mrs Hoysden? "

" Yes. I don't know what made me think of it because she'd been gone for nearly a fortnight, but when I saw him smiling and joking on the phone I didn't think it was her. Still, I couldn't help being a little curious, so while he was still on the phone I went in. He was just finishing talking. ' All right, ten o'clock,' he said and put the receiver down. Then another funny thing happened. Just as we were going to close he said, ' Oh, Louise, I want one of those small tape-recorders, if you don't mind.'"

" Quite cheerfully? "

" Oh, quite. He sounded more casual than anything. That's what made me think afterwards when I heard what he wanted it for. So I got one out and he took it, just like that."

" You didn't notice where he went? "

" Well, I *did* as it happened. To get to his flat from here you have to go out in the street, then in at the main entrance to the block. After I'd locked up I was just in time to see him going in."

" I see. Where did he keep his car? "

" There's a parking place round the back of the block. But I couldn't say whether it was there that evening."

" You didn't see him again? "

" No. Not that evening. Well, never if it comes to that. It wasn't till Sunday evening that I heard about it, then one of the people who live near us in Gaitskell Road happened to mention something she'd heard, and I ran round to the call box and rang Mr Toffin and he told me. I nearly fainted when I heard."

" Would you mind telling me what you did on Saturday evening? "

71

"I can't think why you want to know but as a matter of fact I went to the pictures. I'm not much of a one for the telly though we have it at home."

"Did you go alone?"

"Now that *is* asking. Still I don't see why I shouldn't say. I went with a gentleman who's nothing to do with the business or anything like that."

"You are quite sure you did not see or hear from Mr Hoysden again that evening?"

Miss Hipps stared.

"Quite sure," she said at last. "Now I'd better go and see how Mr Toffin is managing because we seem to be quite busy this morning."

She coiled her way out of the office.

8

CAROLUS found Rupert Priggley the only customer in the Saloon of the Norfolk Hotel, but he had already made the acquaintance of a tall, dissatisfied-seeming, young woman behind the bar. The corners of her mouth turned down and she wore thick glasses.

"She's not quite so sour as she looks, are you, my sweet? And she's full of interesting information about the Drumbone ménage. I told her you're press and I'm telly. Have a drink?"

"I don't know where they get their manners nowadays," said the barmaid grumpily, as she gave Carolus his drink.

"Manners? Isn't that what they had in the Deep South before the Civil War? What was that you were telling me about Mr Rothsay?"

"Only that I don't care for anyone like that."

"See a lot of him?"

"He comes in here, that's all."

" When was he here last? "

" Oh, not for some time."

" Not Saturday night? "

" Not that I noticed. I can't say I'm all that interested."

Carolus asked if she knew Mrs Hoysden by sight.

" Yes. That's the one that used to come in with Mr Rothsay. Stuck-up-looking thing. I've no time for anyone of that sort."

" Was she here on Saturday? "

" I seem to think she was. Just before Closing. But on her own—not with Mr Rothsay."

Carolus asked her to have a drink.

" Thank you," she said without a smile, giving herself a gin-and-tonic. " It's rather early but I'll make an exception."

" Her name's Hilda," explained Rupert Priggley. " Well, it would be, wouldn't it? "

" Do you know any of the Bournes? " asked Carolus.

" The solicitor has a drink here sometimes. I've no use for that sort of man."

" He seemed very harmless."

" Oh, I dare say. Then his young brother comes in with the girl that works for Lady Drumbone, only they don't use this bar. They sit in a corner of the lounge and let the waiter take their drinks in. He used to come in here at one time but seems to want to keep out of the way now. Makes me tired, anything like that. Besides, he's full of talk."

" Really? "

" All about the repertory theatre he was going to start and the exhibition of his pictures and I don't know what. It used to get me down. I was glad when he stopped coming in here."

" Did you know Richard Hoysden himself? "

" I haven't seen him for a long time, not since he got married. I can't say I cared for him much."

" You don't seem to be an enthusiast for the family."

"Oh, I dare say they're all right. Only you get to see

73

another side of people in a place like this. There's not many who come in here I want to bother with, really. Not outside business hours."

"I wonder what you are interested in?"

The corners of the mouth sank lower.

"Well, there's not a lot, is there?" said the barmaid summarizing her arid philosophy.

"A dampening girl," said Priggley as they went to the dining-room for lunch. "What have we got this afternoon?"

"Odds and ends," Carolus told him. "The porter at the block of flats where Hoysden lived and if possible the neighbours who are supposed to have heard the shot."

"Isn't it about time we found that corpse, if there is one?"

"Think so? The inquest is tomorrow. You can go to that. At least there you can scarcely start dancing."

"I was only trying a couple of steps with that redhead."

Though the printed menu was in contrast to that of his dinner of the previous evening, Carolus found it as unexhilarating. It was headed Olde Englisshe Fayre and consisted of tomato soup, grilled cod steaks, roast beef (boiled, then baked, then cut cold and served covered with hot brown cornflour sauce). A vanilla ice triumphantly brought up the rear.

"You know, sir," said Priggley, "I should be the last to criticize, but I can't help wondering whether this is quite the fascinating case you seem to think. What have you got? An uninteresting corpse, this hag Drumbone whose name stinks, a rather drearily united family, a bit of adultery and a rather squalidly sentimental love affair. Chorus of shop-assistants. You'll never get anywhere much with a lot like that."

"I find it, for various reasons which haven't occurred to you, the most interesting case I've had."

"When is something going to happen?"

"What do you mean by 'happen'?"

"You know perfectly well. You say we're going to see a

hall-porter and the tenants of the flats above Hoysden's. That's not very blood-curdling, is it?"

"I don't know how you look at it. I've heard things which are 'blood-curdling', as you call it, in what seem the most commonplace conversations. I heard one this morning. What's more, you may as well know that the people I'm going to see today are only a beginning. We have Hoysden's housekeeper yet, Alan Bourne's sister Olivia Romary, his wife Anita and above all his son Charles described as 'eighteen, spotty and opinionated'. Then there's the young lover Keith and the somewhat older lover Sandy Rothsay. Can't afford to skip any of those."

"But suppose Drumbone's right and Hoysden had only an illusion that he had killed someone?"

"I don't think it was an illusion."

"You can't be sure. And if it was the whole thing will be a frightful waste of time and we shall have spent days in this new town eating Olde Englisshe Fayre for nothing. I wish you'd taken that New Cross case. It sounded like a snorter."

"Patience. Things have a way of developing when you least expect it."

But the first sight of Mr Slugley, the hall-porter, or as he called himself the janitor, of the block of flats over Hoysden's music shop, promised no development at all. He was a large torpid man who absently picked his teeth with a match and with liverish eyes watched the road while he was speaking instead of looking back at his interlocutor.

"Yers . . ." he said absently. "I was on duty that Sat'd'y. Why?"

"I wondered whether you noticed anything," said Carolus.

"Not to say notice, no, I can't say I did. But what was there to notice? That's what I'd like to know. I asked the police that. What was I expected to notice? I asked them." Mr Slugley paused to yawn. "They said 'anything unusual'. There was nothing unusual. Not that I saw, anyway."

Carolus was too experienced a catechist to let it go at this.

"Was there much coming and going?"

"There's always coming and going. You have to get used to it. But that evening there was nothing out of the way. I've got to know most of them that comes, whether they live in the block or are just visitors, and so far as I could see there wasn't one I hadn't seen before."

"Did you know any of them as visitors to Mr Hoysden?"

"No. I can't say I did. He hasn't had a lot of visitors since his wife's gone off and left him."

"What time did he come in that evening?"

"Now that I can't tell you. Unless he slipped in when I wasn't noticing it must have been before eight o'clock when I came on duty. I never saw him that evening at all. Nor did Mr White who was on before me, because the police asked him, too."

There, it seemed, a dead end had been reached, and Priggley moved impatiently. But Carolus stood his ground. And sure enough, after another yawn, while his yellowish eyes were still dully directed to the street scene, Mr Slugley spoke again.

"There was only one could have been to Mr Hoysden's flat. That was this schoolboy."

Carolus knew better than to ask 'which schoolboy?' The identification, suggested as antecedent by 'this', would follow in due course.

"I didn't think it worth mentioning to the police. To tell you the truth I've only just thought of it. It may be nothing to do with anything."

"I should hardly think that."

"It seemed rather funny at the time. See, there's a room at the back where one of us sleeps at night. The company's very particular about that. Must always be one of us on the premises. It's just between the back entrance and the tradesmen's lift. The back entrance is locked at night just before I go off duty at eleven. That night it can't have been long after half-past ten when I could see there wasn't much doing, so I thought I might as well lock up and go to my room at the back for a read of the paper. I'd just gone out there to find my keys and was having a look at the cricket when I heard the service lift on the move downwards from the first floor. I thought that's funny at this time of night, but didn't pay much attention till it stopped and someone got out and opened the back door which is on to the car park. I thought I might as well just see who it was so I put my paper down and had a look. He was half-way across the car park before I'd got the door open, but we keep a light on out there till eleven, and I could see it was a boy from the Grammar School. I know their cap, see? "

" A big boy? "

" Yers. Tall as what you are, I should say, with one arm in a sling."

" Dark glasses? "

" Yers, now you mention it I believe he had."

" You did not know him? "

" No. They all look the same to me. I couldn't tell one from another."

" Were any of them in the habit of coming here? "

" Never see one in the place "

" You would fix the time as soon aften ten-thirty? "

" Between half-past ten and quarter to eleven, anyway."

" You had no reason for thinking he came from Mr Hoysden's flat? "

" Yers, in a way. The lift came from the first floor and there are only six flats there. Gables and Killicks are both away on holiday. Old Mrs Benton-Culverly's in bed by nine and her companion's nearly as old as she is. You wouldn't catch them having schoolboys in the flat at half-past ten—too mean, they are, apart from anything else. Don't seem to know anyone's here, even at Christmastime. I said to . . ."

" And the other two flats? "

" Mrs Jacobs is seriously ill. They say she can't be moved, even to hospital. She's got nurses there all the time. One of them's always wanting something. Then the last flat is a young couple. She's just had a baby. It's her first, and you know what that means."

"No. I'm afraid I've no experience."

Mr Slugley withdrew the match from the cavity he had been exploring in the third molar of the upper jaw.

"Then I'll tell you what it means because I've got five. It means that they don't think or talk of nothing else, nor have anyone near except to take a peep at it; it means you're up half the night with it, and if you do happen to doze off your wife's shaking you to ask if it isn't time for baby to have something or other. It means . . . well, anyhow it means that you wouldn't have no schoolboy in your flat at half-past ten at night unless he was one of the family, which he wasn't, because they've only just come to live here from Newcastle and don't know a soul in the place."

"I see. So you think this mysterious schoolboy with his arm in a sling had been to see Mr Hoysden?"

"Looks like it, doesn't it?"

"I suppose it does. Tell me, does the car park come under your supervision?"

"Not as part of my work it doesn't. I've got quite enough to do as it is. But I do take a look round it every now'n again. It so happens I'm interested in cars. Always have been."

Carolus suppressed his surprise that Slugley was interested in anything and asked: "Did you happen to go out there during the evening?"

"Yers. I did have a look once. Why?"

"What time would that have been?"

"Oh, I couldn't say, not to the minute. It was after nine. I should say between nine and half-past."

"All in order?"

"Yers. Same as usual. Except there was one car I noticed particularly because it was a Mercedes. We don't often get one of them."

"You didn't see its owner?"

"No. But very likely he didn't come in here at all.

78

There's the Fox and Hounds just across the way, and I've often seen them use our car park while they go in there. They've no business to, but I don't say anything. I've got enough to do."

"I'm very much obliged to you." A ten-shilling note flickered for a moment and disappeared as though a conjuror's success depended on its quick concealment. "Now can you tell me which tenants it was who told the police they had heard the shot?"

"Yers. But I don't know as it will be much use to you. They're both pretty shaky about it, though one's all talk and the other don't say much. The police went to every flat in the building where the people aren't away, but these was the only two they got anything from. They're both on the second floor funnily enough. No one on the same floor as Mr Hoysden heard anything at all. Still you can go. You might be able to make something of it. They're the Nodges in number 21 and Hoskinses in 23. I don't know whether any of them are in now but you can try."

The lift in this block was even swifter than in Drumbone House, and Carolus felt like something being launched from the Woomera range. A little dizzily he sought number 21 and rang the bell.

A bright blonde woman in a yellow overall opened the door and looked like a huge canary.

"Is it about Downstairs?" she asked at once, "Because my husband says we don't want any more reporters after that picture they published of him in an apron."

"I'm not a reporter," said Carolus. Then, deciding to chance it, added, "I'm acting for Lady Drumbone."

"I don't know what to say. What is it you want to know?"

"Only about the shot," said Carolus.

"I suppose you'd better come in, though there's not much to tell, and I've got some friends coming to play bridge in a minute. We heard it quite distinctly, bang, like that. I said 'I believe that was a shot', but my husband would have it it was was a car back-firing."

79

"Did you notice the time?"

"That's what the police wanted to know. We've gone over it again and again and can't be sure. But it wasn't before half-past ten and not after eleven-fifteen. That's all I can tell you. Of course I never dreamt at the time it was poor Mr Hoysden. Otherwise we should have gone down."

"You knew him, then?"

"Just to say good-morning to. But we shouldn't let that stand in the way in case of someone shooting himself. I noticed at the time it sounded sort of muffled as though it came from inside the building, but my husband said no, it was outside. So there you are."

"You heard nothing more?"

"Then, you mean? No. But it was a funny thing I must have dreamed about the shot because I woke up in the night and could have sworn I heard it. I can tell you what time that was because I turned the light on to take an aspirin and it was ten minutes to four. But my husband said I'd got shots on the brain—he hadn't heard anything and wanted to get to sleep."

"Thank you, Mrs Nodges. Do the police know about that second shot?"

"Oh, I don't suppose it was any more than me dreaming, really. I never mentioned it. My husband said, 'Don't, for goodness' sake. People will think you're not right in the head if you go on talking about shots.' So this is the first time I've said anything. But it was funny, wasn't it?"

"Yes," replied Carolus in time to stop Priggley saying 'screamingly'.

"Then if you want to know any more you'd better go and see Mr Hoskins, though you'll find he's quiet. Very quiet, indeed. It's as much as any of us can do to get a word out of him, though *she* talks for the two of them when she's here. She's away now and you'll find him alone, if he's in. My husband calls him the hermit crab."

"Thank you once again."

Carolus was relieved to find that preparations for her bridge party kept Mrs Nodges from following his movements and he rang the bell of 23 unobserved.

Mr Hoskins came himself to the door, a tall, thin man with a long, sad face. He seemed to realize the tactical advantages of silence in the face of an intruder, for he stood there without speaking and waited for Carolus to explain himself.

" Mr Hoskins? "

The long, thin lips opened scarcely at all to emit an abridged North-country sound.

" Ay," said Mr Hoskins.

" I'm investigating the matter of Richard Hoysden's death, on behalf of Lady Drumbone. Could I have a few words with you? "

" Ay," said Mr Hoskins, but did not move from his stance in the doorway.

" I understand you heard the shot? "

Hoskins showed no emotion.

" Ay," he answered.

" What time would that have been? "

Priggley whispered ' Got him this time ' and waited. But Priggley was wrong. Mr Hoskins only shrugged his shoulders. As if resigned to playing Twenty Questions with a taciturn question-master, Carolus said " Would it have been after ten-thirty? "

" Ay," said Mr Hoskins, back on safe ground.

" Before eleven? "

Mr Hoskins surprised them both with his loquacity.

" Couldn't say."

He showed no impatience to shut the door however, seeming resigned to such chatty interludes.

" Did you hear anything else that night? "

Mr Hoskins shook his head.

" You are, perhaps, a heavy sleeper? "

" Ay."

" And you were alone that night? "

" Ay."

"You would have heard it if there had been another shot?"

Carolus and Priggley waited breathlessly. They were rewarded by two syllables.

"There weren't," said Mr Hoskins.

"But if you sleep heavily and it was in the small hours?"

"There weren't," repeated Mr Hoskins.

"Did you know Richard Hoysden?"

"Ay."

Carolus was about to say 'intimately?' when he realized the absurdity of the question to Mr Hoskins.

"See much of him?"

This caused a hold-up. At last Mr Hoskins found a single word to explain what, for most of us, would necessitate a hundred at least.

"Music," he said.

"Oh, you shared his interest in music and perhaps heard it together. Was there a particular programme that night?"

"Ay. Beethoven's Trio in E Minor," said Mr Hoskins in an unprecedented burst of loquacity.

"And did you go down to Hoysden's flat to listen?"

Mr Hoskins shook his head.

"You did not see him at all that evening?"

Again a slow head-shake.

"But you think he listened to a certain programme?"

"Ay."

"He had told you he intended to?"

"Ay."

Carolus decided to look up Saturday's programmes to see the time of this one rather than become involved in further conversational exchanges with Mr Hoskins.

"I'm very much obliged to you," he said, and found that unconsciously, as though talking to someone hard of hearing, his voice had grown louder and louder as he battled with the other's monosyllables.

"I'm not deaf," said Mr Hoskins.

Carolus did not trust himself to answer.

82

9

"No more today," pleaded Priggley.

"Ay," said Carolus, making for the stairs rather than the lift.

"*Not* the schoolboy? *Not* Alan Bourne's home?"

"Ay," said Carolus relentlessly.

"It's too much," said Priggley. "I shall throw up."

"Hang on while I telephone," Carolus said when they were outside the building, for the new town of Maresfield had telephone booths like sentries at most street-corners.

He returned smiling.

"We're invited to tea by Anita Bourne," he said.

The family lived in one of the houses which the planners of the new town had left from the old, choosing, for preservation, a group of hideous Victorian villas. Mount Edgcumbe had bay windows, a conservatory, Portugal laurels, asphalt paths, geraniums, sun-blinds and ornamental trees which Carolus suspected of being laburnums. The door was opened by a middle-aged woman whose appearance and manner were somewhere between those of a servant and a member of the family.

She showed them into a room with so much chintz and displayed silver and smell of camphor that it could only be called 'the drawing-room'.

"Anita obviously means to make an entrance," said Priggley.

This was an understatement. Mrs Bourne when she came in seemed to be awaiting a round of applause.

"Miss-ter Deene!" she cried. "I have been expecting you! When my husband told me you had taken up our tragedy, I said 'Ah, now we shall know the truth about poor Richard.' Any information I can give is yours, I need scarcely say."

"Thank you. Is your son in?"

" My son? Charles? I can scarcely imagine any connection which he, a mere schoolboy, might have with this, but of course if he can tell you anything he will. He is in, yes. But pray let me ring for tea."

It was many years since Carolus had heard that Edwardian phrase and it recalled starched caps and aprons. The middle-aged person who had opened the door brought in a tray but said "Where will you have it?" in a most unmenial way.

Then Charles appeared—with his arm in a sling. He was, as Carolus had been warned, spotty, but seemed too nervous to be self-opinionated.

Carolus and Priggley were placed at some distance from Mrs Bourne, so would have to balance cups and plates on the arms of their chairs, for their hostess evidently meant to show that she knew how to do things. Charles was told to hand round their cups after ceremonious questions about sugar and 'cream' had been asked and answered.

Mrs Bourne was pretentiously dressed and had a carefully cultivated speaking voice; the sort of affected and languishing woman one expected to talk about things being U and Non-U.

" And now," she said almost simperingly, " What are you going to ask me, Mr Deene? I am ready for the ordeal."

Carolus turned to the schoolboy son who had his mouth full of cake.

" What's the matter with your arm?" he asked, rather peremptorily.

Mrs Bourne answered for Charles, who looked rather confused.

" The silly boy fell off his bicycle," she said. " Dr Stott says he is lucky not to have broken his wrist."

" When did this happen?" Carolus looked straight at Charles.

" Last Friday," he said sulkily.

" Only he did not tell me till Saturday morning. I sent him to Dr Stott at once and he dressed it."

" Was that before you called at the shop, or after? " asked Carolus.

Mrs Bourne turned to Charles.

" What shop, darling? " she asked. " I didn't know you did any shopping on Saturday."

" Richard Hoysden's shop," said Carolus.

" Before," said Charles. " I had half an hour before I was due at the surgery."

" You were alone with Richard? "

" I was talking to him."

" What about? "

" I forget now."

" Does it matter? " asked his mother. " Lots of people talked to Richard after Charles did, I'm sure."

" It matters a great deal," said Carolus. " Were you discussing what you owed him? "

" I don't . . ."

" Charles, dear, you never told me about this," said Mrs Bourne reproachfully.

" It was only some records I had," said Charles.

" You didn't get the saxophone, then? "

" Saxophone! " said Mrs Bourne. Then quickly recovering—" But what has all this to do with poor Richard's suicide, Mr Deene? You are not suggesting that he killed himself because my son had some dealings with his shop? "

" Now would you mind telling me what you were discussing with Richard that morning? " asked Carolus pointedly of Charles, ignoring his mother.

" Only about that. He told me to ask Dad first."

" Very natural," commented Mrs Bourne.

" Then, that evening? "

" I don't know what you mean," said Charles.

" What time did you go to Richard's flat? "

" Charles! "

" I never went," said Charles.

" Where did you go? "

" To the pictures."

" Alone? "

" Yes."

" And afterwards? "

" I walked about a bit. Then came home."

" What time? "

" About eleven."

" Meet anyone you knew? "

" Not that I remember."

" You didn't go anywhere near Richard's flat? "

" I may have passed by there. I didn't go in."

" You didn't leave by the service door of the block some time after ten-thirty? "

" No."

" You wore your school cap that evening? "

" Yes. Dad likes me to. Even in the holidays."

" And sun-glasses? "

" He has to wear sun-glasses, Mr Deene. The oculist . . ."

" You had them on that evening? "

" I suppose so."

" I think you would find it best to tell me the truth," said Carolus.

" That is the truth."

" This is really very extraordinary, Mr Deene. Your cross-examining my son in this way. What possible connection can he have with Richard's suicide? "

" I can only assure you that on his word depends almost everything," said Carolus.

Charles looked sulky.

" Do tell Mr Deene anything you know, dear."

" I have."

Carolus tried again, more patiently.

" What did you do that afternoon? "

" Went to tea with Aunt Olivia," said Charles.

" He's devoted to his aunt," said Mrs Bourne.

" Was anyone else there? "

" Only Keith came in for a minute."

" Richard didn't? "

" Not while I was there."

" You didn't at any time see Pippa Hoysden? "

"No. I didn't know she was in the town till afterwards. I saw Rothsay. Driving down the High Street in an open car."

"What time?"

"Soon after the pictures."

"Did he see you?"

"Yes. He waved."

"You know him well?"

"No. Pippa introduced me once in the Carmona Café."

"Surely, Mr Deene," said Mrs Bourne, "you have all the information you can possibly require from my son. Let me give you some more tea."

"No, thank you. I must go."

"But . . . is there nothing you want to ask me?"

"Nothing, thanks."

"How very extraordinary! I naturally thought it would be me you would question."

"On what subject?"

"Richard's character, of course. And the unfortunate affair of Pippa and this Rothsay man."

"It's very kind of you. I'm sure you would have a great deal to say. There is one small matter about which I should like to ask you, Mrs Bourne."

"And that?"

"The revolver used by Richard."

There was a very awkward silence. Carolus might have produced a revolver and pointed it instead of mentioning one. When Mrs Bourne spoke she seemed to have forgotten the practised modulations of her voice.

"Are you mad? Asking *me* about a revolver!"

"No, Mrs Bourne. I'm not mad. I think you may be able to help me about this. Have you ever seen a revolver in Richard's possession?"

"Certainly not."

"When did you last see a revolver of any sort?"

"I . . . my husband has one."

"Where does he keep it?"

"Locked in a drawer in our bedroom."

"When did you see it last?"

"Oh, years ago. This is absurd, Mr Deene."

"Not really. Is it still there?"

"Of course."

"How do you know?"

"It must be. The drawer has not been broken into."

"But the locks of drawers have a way of being old-fashioned standard things which almost any key of that size will open."

"You mean you think Richard may have taken Alan's revolver?"

"I mean, I should like very much to see if it is still there."

Mrs Bourne was silent for a moment.

"I think we should wait for my husband to come in. He won't be long."

"As you wish."

"No need for me to wait, is there, Mother?" asked Charles, who had begun to fidget like a very small boy.

"No, dear, no."

From the windows of the drawing-room Charles could be seen making for the front gate. He had soon disappeared.

A difficult ten minutes followed. Mrs Bourne talked in a voice which Rupert Priggley afterwards described, not altogether without justice, as 'tarty'. She spoke of the 'commonness' of some neighbours, the 'niceness' of others; how she did not associate' with the first and 'occasionally entertained' the second; how her daughter was at one of the nicest of girls' schools and was spending part of the holiday with her friend the daughter of a Second Secretary. But when these topics were exhausted Mrs Bourne returned to the surprises of Carolus's visit.

"The way you grilled that poor son of mine, Mr Deene!" she said archly. "Really, one would think he was an accomplice. Then to ask me questions about a revolver, of all things! Do you really think poor Richard can have got hold of my husband's?"

Carolus was saved from answering this question by the

hurried entrance of Alan Bourne who seemed to be feeling the heat or some violent emotion.

"I have just met my son," he said loudly to Carolus without any preliminary greeting, "and he has told me of your questions about my revolver. Are you serious in asking about it?"

"Quite," said Carolus.

"Do I understand that you suggest that it may have been the one used by Richard?"

"I have suggested nothing. I simply asked if it was still in its usual place."

"Perhaps you had forgotten that it was I who found my cousin's body? Do you think I shouldn't have recognized my own revolver?"

"You'd have recognized it all right."

"Then you accuse me of withholding evidence?"

"I haven't accused you of anything, yet. I asked whether your revolver is in its place. There is nothing to get excited about. You intended to withhold evidence, as you put it, about the recording. Why not about the revolver?"

"That's rather cheek, Deene."

"Yes, I'm afraid it was. Let's all keep cool, shall we? Your revolver might have been taken, you know, and you might, understandably, have not wished to admit it. It might even be unlicensed. At all events, I should have asked you and not Mrs Bourne about it."

Alan Bourne sat down.

"Yes. I think you should," he said more calmly.

"Perhaps, though, to settle the whole thing we might just confirm that it is still there?"

Bourne tried to smile.

"When I've had a cup of tea," he said, "I will go upstairs and look, if that will set your mind at rest."

"Thank you," said Carolus.

A moment after Alan Bourne had left the room Priggley whispered mysteriously to his hostess.

"I wonder if I might . . . the lavatory . . ."

"The door facing you in the hall," said Mrs Bourne

shortly, evidently disliking this near-mention of a physical necessity.

Priggley returned in a few moments, but Alan Bourne appeared to be delayed. When he returned he was smiling.

"Exactly as I left it," he said. "Wrapped in a piece of flannel as I always keep it."

"Have you a permit for it?" asked Carolus.

"Of course."

"Then you won't mind the police knowing of its exist--ence?"

"My dear man, they already know of its existence, since they gave me the permit."

"Naturally. I had forgotten that."

"You've rather shaken my confidence, Deene, by all this hu-ha about a revolver."

"Pity. You remember your cousin's words. 'Lucky I've got this revolver. A souvenir.' Did you know he had kept this souvenir?"

"I . . . seem to remember his mentioning it once. I can't be sure."

"You had never seen it?"

"No. No."

"Yours was also a souvenir, I suppose?"

"In a way, yes. I had it during the war."

"Thank you. I'm sorry if I seemed rather insistent. This is an intricate case."

"The point is, are you any nearer to knowing whether or not we are to be faced with a corpse? That is what is troubling my aunt, and all of us. That is why we called you in."

"I don't know," said Carolus. "I simply don't know, yet. I'm afraid it is a distinct possibility, though."

"Poor dear Richard," put in Mrs Bourne. "If he hadn't married that . . ."

Bourne spoke hastily.

"I have told Deene that I don't believe his marriage had anything to do with it."

Carolus took his leave. He felt that Alan Bourne was on

90

the verge of saying something, or was worried about something, or perhaps was feeling the strain of a situation which was trying to all connected with it. But he made no attempt to gain more information now.

"Well?" he said to Priggley when they were in the car.

"He didn't mean to go upstairs at all. I found him waiting in the hall. That means that he knew the revolver wasn't there, doesn't it?"

"Not necessarily. He may have known it *was* there. That would mean he had looked to see quite recently and would be almost as incriminating."

"Of whom?"

"Don't be silly," said Carolus. "We can just make Newminster in time for dinner. Mrs Stick can produce her *riz de veau* at last."

10

If not 'merry as a marriage bell' that evening Mrs Stick was certainly in a more amiable frame of mind. She took advantage of the presence at dinner of both Carolus and Rupert Priggley to produce some of the food she had been hoping to serve yesterday.

"I'm giving you the sweetbreads as an on tray," she said, "then the jiggot afterwards with some jay lay der gross eye roudges."

Carolus smiled.

"You go too far, Mrs Stick. Red currant jelly."

"Well, that's what it's called in the book and I *do* like to be correct, not like those that don't know the proper name for anything. You'll have a bottle of the Ma Gokes with that, won't you, sir?"

But next morning all was confounded. Carolus came down to find Mrs Stick in her most disapproving mood.

"It's begun," she said enigmatically. "There's a person

waiting to see you. Maresfield, his card says. That's where Mr Gorringer says this poor man shot himself."

Carolus rose.

"No, sir, I've got your breakfast all hot for you," said Mrs Stick firmly, "so he can wait till you've had it whatever he's come about."

She stood between Carolus and the door till he had eaten, then reluctantly let him pass.

He found Alan Bourne waiting for him.

"Look here, Deene. This is an awkward matter. I've come over early because the Inquest is today and I have to be there. It's about that revolver."

"It was yours, wasn't it, that Richard used?"

"Well, yes, it was. Only I didn't want it to come out in front of the wife. She gets upset about things."

"Have you told the police?"

"Actually, I haven't. You see you were quite right, I haven't got a permit for it. I recognized it as soon as I found Richard's body, but I said nothing about it. A charge of possessing a firearm without a permit couldn't be made against him then, poor chap, and would be very damaging to me."

"How did you suppose he had got hold of it?"

"That wasn't difficult. As you told my wife yesterday the drawer in a chest-of-drawers can be opened all too easily."

"It had not been forced?"

"No. I've had a good look at it. I should have been more careful, of course. I find now that the same key will open all the drawers in the chest and one of them had the key in it. So anyone could have taken it."

"Anyone who knew it was there. Who did?"

"I expect the whole family."

Carolus was rather tired of hearing about this family.

"When did you miss it?"

"I didn't miss it. I haven't looked at it for years. It was only after I saw it by Richard's bed that I realized. At least I had the sense not to take it away or hide it, or anything. That would have been foolish."

" It would. So Richard himself could have taken it? "

" I suppose so, but I don't know when. He was fairly often at the house but never stayed a night there."

" That is true of the rest of your family? "

" Yes. There's only one possibility that I can think of. We have, as you may have noticed, a tennis-court. This summer we've had several tennis parties and our room has been used for changing and so on."

" By men or women? "

" Both. On different occasions, of course."

" When was the last? "

" Last Friday, actually."

" Who was there? "

" All of us. Richard, Olivia, Keith, even my aunt came, though she did not play."

" Anyone else? "

" Her secretary, Wilma Day."

" Any of Richard's staff? "

" Oh, yes. I was forgetting that. He asked my wife as a favour if he might bring his senior assistants, a man called Toffin and a Miss Hipps."

" I'm glad you've told me about this. I was fairly sure it was your revolver. You'll have to tell the police. If you confide in them and don't wait for them to find out it's yours, I don't think you'll find it very serious."

" But the law . . ."

" My dear Bourne, not for nothing do criminals call the police ' The Law '. If they present the case in the right way to the magistrate you will get a small fine."

" You really think it's necessary? "

" Of course it is."

" You are not coming to the Inquest? "

" I think not. I have never learned anything yet from attending an inquest. The verdict's a foregone conclusion. Suicide while the balance of his mind etcetera."

But when Bourne had left him he suggested to Priggley that he should go over on his motor-cycle and note what details there were.

"I have a feeling," said Carolus, "that they haven't yet admitted the existence of the tape-recording. My bet is that a little family council decided to wait till after the inquest to avoid publicity. Then they will go brightly to the police and say they've only just discovered what it was. So that if no corpse is found the thing will rest there—suicide because his wife had left him—so far as public knowledge is concerned, and the Drumbone will escape any involvement."

"What do you want me to do? Stand up and denounce them?"

"I want you to notice what happens, that's all. I'm going to take a day's holiday from Maresfield."

"To think it over, I suppose? To fit together the pieces of the jig-saw puzzle in the accepted manner? Then when I come home you must look at me enigmatically and say, 'I begin to see light'. So I goggle and say, 'Do you really?' Then you ask some fabulously unexpected question like, 'Has Miss Hipps a pair of tennis shoes . . .'"

"Yes. Has she, by the way? It's rather important."

"Don't give me that, sir. I *wish* you'd read more crime fiction. You've no idea how dated you are. All this looking for clues and questioning suspects and being mysterious about your theory till the last minute—it went out ages ago."

"And what has come in?"

"Sixty thrills to the minute stuff. Death and destruction. Or else frightfully deep psychology. Sinister complexes. Appalling inhibitions. Or else, one further, sheer science fiction. Whatever it is you're becoming just a relic of a by-gone method. A reactionary. Look at you today. 'A day off to think it over . . .'"

"I said nothing about thinking it over. I want a rest from that bedlam of bright new buildings and 'our family life'."

"I see your point. All right. I'll bring you back the dope. What do you want to know from Hoysden's?"

"Nothing."

"I thought I'd take another look at that redhead. And

94

you said you wanted to know about Hipps's tennis shoes."

" Out! " said Carolus and took up *The Times* crossword. What a treat to find that Hollingbourne had not industriously entered two wrong clues. ' Kate with a squeaky voice 5, 5.' Too easy again. He must wait for Sunday's Ximenes.

The trouble was the odious Priggley was right—Carolus *did* want to think it over, and he *did* begin to see the beginnings of a ray of light. If he was right there was no need for haste; there was no more danger to anyone. He could well afford to lounge about and show Mrs Stick that he was resting.

When she came in he said apologetically " That was only a solicitor, Mrs Stick."

" I'm not saying he wasn't, but still he's mixed up in it. Now are you going to be in today? "

" All day."

She looked at him suspiciously as though this was too good to be true.

" I suppose that means they'll be coming here to see you? "'

" Who? "

" Murderers and police and that."

" I don't think anyone will be coming to see me."

" Well, that's something. I can get on with the lunch."

But Carolus was wrong. He had a caller that morning, and a very unexpected one. About half an hour after the departure of Priggley, Mrs Stick with an I-told-you-so expression showed in Detective Inspector John Moore.

Moore was an old friend and had been in charge of two cases in which Carolus was involved. He was burly, efficient and always to the point.

They greeted each other with outward cordiality, but some private reserve. Carolus knew very well that John Moore did not call at eleven o'clock in the morning to pass the time of day, and waited to see what would transpire. After they had smoked and drunk together for ten minutes, Carolus asked the first question.

"Come on," he said, "what have you come to see me about?"

John Moore smiled.

"I was waiting for you to ask that. It's this suicide over at Maresfield."

"But that's not in your manor."

"No. A friend of mine has it. Man called Bowler. Good chap. When he told me you'd been over there I thought it best to give you a call. Quite unofficially, of course."

"Of course."

"Look, Carolus. Keep out of this, will you? There's nothing for you in it. It's suicide, plain and simple."

"It may be suicide," said Carolus. "It isn't plain—or simple."

"Why not? The fellow shot himself. Plenty of cases like that. Weapon found beside him. Finger-prints, direction of shot, all correct. The only thing is there was no final note left to be found near the body. But that's not unusual, either."

Carolus said nothing.

"You see," went on John Moore, "Bowler's satisfied that this was suicide. Quite satisfied. If you start something which stirs up doubt in the mind of the . . . public . . ."

"Press, you were going to say."

"Press, then. We know Drumbone's reputation. Personally I've got no use for her, but the fact that she's *in* this, the dead man's aunt and living in the place, means that it's very easy to start a hare. If it's known that you're investigating and apparently not satisfied with the coroner's verdict, which will come today, rumours will start which nothing can stop. I'm not worried about Drumbone. I just don't want it said again that the police have not done all they could. So do me a favour, Carolus. Lay off it. When there's something in my manor which will interest you, I'll promise to let you know."

"Thanks. You've been frank, so will I. This is the position, John. There's a piece of evidence, a damned, great, black, ugly piece of evidence, which has evidently

96

been kept from the police. That's no fault of mine. The person involved promised to give it to them at once, and I thought that person had, till this morning. It will be handed over immediately after the inquest. If it isn't, when I reach Maresfield tomorrow I'll see that it is. When your man has this he will take a different view of the case. I can say no more than that."

They exchanged looks. John Moore was satisfied that nothing could be gained by further talk at present.

"You might have known me better," said Carolus less seriously, "than to think I'd waste time on a straight-forward suicide with no strings attached."

"It surprised me, I must say. You might have been a friend of the family."

"Don't talk to me about 'the family'. Perhaps, in a sense I was wrong just now. It wasn't one piece of evidence but two. They should both be in your hands today."

"I see."

"There's one thing though, John. Give me your man's private address, will you? Bowler's, I mean. I might need to see him in a hurry."

John Moore wrote it down. When he had left, Carolus deliberately put the case out of his mind until Priggley's return. He delighted Mrs Stick by remaining at home, even going to 'have a word' with Stick in the walled garden. 'Stick was ever so pleased,' reported his wife later, though Carolus was unable, as usual, to detect any emotion in the man.

The day, in fact, passed all too quickly till Carolus heard the din of Rupert's motor-cycle.

"Hoysden's was closed," were Rupert's first irritating words.

"Naturally. Toffin's evidence was wanted."

"I thought I'd take another look at that redhead."

"You went to attend an inquest."

"Oh, yes, the inquest. You were quite right. Nothing was said about the recording, which must mean they haven't handed it over."

" Damned fools."

" I don't think it would have made much difference to the verdict. Everyone seemed to have decided about that from the start. I had the impression that it was all being toned down to avoid fuss and publicity. Drumbone was not called. The whole thing was made to sound very commonplace—proprietor of music shop, private worries, neurotic as result of war service, unhappy marriage, shoots himself in a fit of insane depression."

" What about the unhappy marriage? "

" Not stressed. Pippa was questioned. Nothing seriously wrong between them. Often had little tiffs. Everyone nodded sympathetically."

" Nice and cosy," said Carolus.

" There were some more difficult moments. Wait till you see the housekeeper, Mrs Tuck. She's what they call a Tartar. She stirred them up a bit. ' I should think you *did* want to know! ' she told the coroner. ' And you're not the only one. Everybody was going to have everything after the bombing stopped, wasn't they? Well, this is what you've brought him to, all the lot of you. Had to shoot himself because he couldn't stand any more of it, and I don't blame him.' She didn't explain what ' it ' might be, but I think I understood."

" Who else gave evidence? "

" Toffin. ' Always-a-perfect-gentleman ' line. Had Richard business worries? Not so far as the shop was concerned, but Toffin thought he might have had what he called ' private business worries '. He gave the impression that in business Richard was little better than a half-wit and that he, Toffin, was a genius. Were the shop finances in order? He ' flattered himself ' that under any kind of scrutiny they were impeccable. Richard knew that, and had frequently thanked Toffin for his care.

" Then they had something called Hipps to give evidence. Floods of tears. She wanted to give the impression that Richard had pursued her for years, but she only succeeded in making herself look like a pining King Charles spaniel. Repulsive exhibition, and she had nothing to add."

"What about my friends from upstairs?"

"Mrs Nodges did her act. She's got it by heart, now, including the bit about 'bang, like that'. Mr Hoskins gave his impersonation of a North-country oyster, till the coroner began saying 'Ay' and had to correct himself. Slugley was called—no mention of the schoolboy."

"What about Olivia Romary?"

"Not called. But I tell you whose evidence did provide something new—the blonde who was in that bungalow at Marling Flats. She is Wilma Day, the Drumbone's secretary, but that was not mentioned. Her evidence was that Richard had met her as she came out of Drumbone House that evening—about 7.20 they think—and offered her a lift. As she knew him already (point much emphasized), she accepted and he drove her to the station from which she was going to see her mother for the week-end."

"So he did go out that evening."

"Apparently."

"Anyone else?"

"Alan Bourne. You'll be interested to know that he dropped a real clanger. About that revolver."

"He hadn't told the police?"

"Shouldn't think so, judging from his face when the coroner asked him if he'd ever seen the revolver before. What could he say? He muttered 'yes' and tried to go on about something else."

"But?"

"But the coroner was no fool. 'To whom did this revolver belong?' he asked very clearly. Bourne looked as thought he was trying to swallow his Adam's apple. 'It was mine,' he said at last. That kept him in the witness-box for another half-hour. Where was it kept? Who could have taken it? He gave the names of all the guests at his Friday afternoon tennis-party, including some 'nice' friends of his wife's we didn't know about. I must say he looked pretty sick."

"So would you if you were a solicitor about to be charged with possessing arms without a permit."

"Is that all they'll charge him with?" asked Priggley in obvious disappointment.

"It's enough," said Carolus.

11

"BACK to the grindstone," said Carolus next morning. "I can't stay away from Maresfield another day."

"If you're going to see Mrs Tuck, I'm coming," said Rupert Priggley.

"I am. And Olivia Romary. They should finish the locals. I'll ask Keith here, I think, and put you out of the way. I don't want any of your acid comments when he tells me of love's young dream."

"Suits me," said Rupert. "I had quite enough of that at Marling Flats. 'Darling, darling'."

Mrs Tuck lived in a bright new house, one of several hundred constructed in artfully irregular pattern in an area called an estate. She had been described by Alan Bourne as ferocious, and when she first came to the door she might have been an aged and mangy tigress disturbed in her cage by the prodding stick of small boys.

"I've told you a dozen times I don't want household appliances, television, radio, carpet sweepers, grocery or washing machines!" she shouted furiously. "I don't believe in hire purchase, and the next time any of your lot come around I'll set the dog on you."

"I . . ."

"Don't argue with me because I mean what I say. I've had enough of it. I've got plenty to do without opening the door every five mintes."

"It's not . . ."

"What is it then? I've paid my rent and rates, dog

licence, health insurance, wireless licence, television licence, union, electric light, gas, house insurance, and water rate. Perhaps you've thought of something new, have you? If so you can tell Them I'm not paying any more. I'd rather go to prison than put up with it. Forms and stamps! It's enough to drive anyone out of their senses."

" I assure you . . ."

" Nor I won't vote for any of Them, so tell Them that. They're all as bad as the other. Not for the Town Council nor for Parliament either. You tell Them. I don't care which party gets elected to what. You can have the lot of them so far as I'm concerned. *And* the British Commonwealth *and* the Royal Family. All the lot."

" Mrs Tuck . . ."

" And if you've come from one of those opinion polls you can clear off double-quick. Do I think this, or do I think that. I don't think, I *know* that They've made the country so's it's not fit to live in. I hate the whole boiling of Them. Tell Them that, if you want my opinion."

" Mr Hoysden . . ." shouted Carolus desperately.

" What about Mr Hoysden? There's another one They did for with their bloody forms and stamps and what you must do and what you mustn't do. I'm not surprised he shot himself. I'd do it, too, only I'd like to shoot a few of Them first."

" I want to ask you about Mr Hoysden, Mrs Tuck."

Mrs Tuck's face, hitherto a mere scarlet, turned a rich purple.

" If you're a copper," she began, but this time it was Carolus who interrupted.

" I'm not! " he yelled.

" Well, what are you then? I told the coroner yesterday what I thought, and I'd tell him again even if They lock me up for it. What do They think people are? "

" I've often wondered," said Carolus, " not people, anyway. Perhaps you'll listen long enough for me to tell you what I want? I want to know the truth about Richard Hoysden. I've heard that tape-recording. I think the whole case is an extraordinary one. I think you can help me. I'm not an official of any kind and I don't like Them any more than you do."

Mrs Tuck stared at him for a moment.

"Come in!" she ordered.

Carolus followed her.

"They don't like me round here," she said, "because I believe in speaking my mind. You must excuse this place, but They pulled down our old cottage which had belonged to my husband's father when They built these. It was a bit damp I dare say, but you had got room to turn round. There we had a decent bit of garden with an old bullace tree that gave me enough jam to last the year round. Here They won't even let you grow what you like. Can you imagine that? It has to be lawn in the front same as all the others, or They turn you out. My husband wanted to climb a wistaria over the house like we used to have, but They said no. Now what do you want to know about Mr Hoysden?"

"Anything you feel like telling me."

"Well, they was all after him. The family, I mean. He was the only one who could have been independent if he'd of wanted to. He didn't have to run to Her whenever he wanted anything. She helped him start the shop . . ."

"You mean Lady Drumbone, of course?"

"Yes. I mean Her. She helped him start, but he paid all that back long ago. The rest of them didn't like that. But Richard never showed his independence. He was always very respectful to Her. More than what I'd have been."

"Why do you think he shot himself?" asked Carolus, who feared Mrs Tuck's recollections might be somewhat general.

"Why would anyone, nowadays? You can't really wonder the way things are going, can you? Ordered about like sheep all the time. I suppose he'd just had enough of it, like anyone might have. It's all right for those that want to be like everyone else. Soon as you've got any ideas of your own you're done for. Like my son. He didn't know

102

himself what he wanted, but it had to be a bit different. He was a good boy to me and his dad, but he got in with the wrong lot and now They've sent him to Borstal. I don't say it was right, what he did, but They made him like that. Now I suppose he'll never go straight."

"Did Richard Hoysden want to be different?"

"He was always one to say people should lead their own lives, and that's what you mustn't do nowadays. He used to say to me, 'I like you, Mrs Tuck, because you go your own way.' Not in the work, he didn't mean. Work's work, and I did mine the way they wanted it. But I won't be told to walk here and stop there. Very soon we shall all be marched everywhere like soldiers. Richard was easy-going up to a point, but it's my belief he thought a lot more than he said, and just couldn't stand it any more."

"Then how do you account for the recording?"

"I don't know what to think. It'll seem silly to you, perhaps, but I can't help half wondering if he did it for a sort of joke. To lead Them on, see, and give Them something to think about. Perhaps partly to take Them off believing it was anything to do with Pippa. I don't know. I can't explain it any other way."

"You don't think he imagined he'd killed someone?"

"No. I don't. Not Richard. Unless he really went out of his mind, which I can't believe, either."

The door bell rang.

"Half a minute," said Mrs Tuck, and pulling out a handkerchief she deftly inserted it between the clapper and the bell. "Let them ring. It's only another of these bloody salesmen trying to tie you up for the rest of your life for an electric iron. Or else an inspector from the Council wanting to see how we keep the house inside. Do you wonder he did for himself? There's never a moment's peace." There was a loud knocking. "Hark at that! He wants to look at all the meters in the place by the sound of it, though they only came last week. Or else it's about the health insurance. Let 'em knock. There's nothing like a building estate for peace and quiet, I can tell you. You can't do anything about it, either. If you drop so much as a bucket of water on them you're in court and very likely sent to prison. You ask me why Richard Hoysden shot himself. Because he lived in Maresfield, that's why. If you lived here you'd understand."

"He never said anything to you which made you think he was considering it?"

"No. We didn't talk a lot. But I knew. The way he used to say 'Hell!' Lots of little things. He'd had enough of it."

Mrs Tuck went to a cupboard and pulled out an unlabelled bottle.

"Cowslip wine," she said. "They'll think of a way of stopping you making this soon. You'll see. Anything you like doing's bound to be wrong. That's what my son used to say."

Without a direct invitation she poured out three glassfuls. It was of startling strength and flavour.

"There's only one other thing I can tell you," said Mrs Tuck, "someone had been to Richard's flat between when I left at four o'clock on Saturday and when I got there on Sunday morning."

"Alan Bourne," said Carolus.

"No, not him. Someone else. I picked a little comb up off the floor of the bedroom."

"How do you know it wasn't Alan Bourne's?"

"Because I asked him there and then and he said no. I pretended I thought it was Richard's, but I knew it wasn't. Richard's was in his pocket. I saw the things the police found on him before they took him away. I'll show it to you."

She opened her bag and handed Carolus a red comb.

"Might be a man's or a woman's," she said. "There's nothing to tell. It was on the floor not far from where the pistol was."

"Pity you didn't tell the police. It must have been smothered in finger-prints."

"Oh, I don't believe in all that. That's how they got

my son. You can keep it now if you like. It may help you to find out something. I've never said anything about it."

"Thanks," said Carolus. Examining it, he asked: "Did you ever know Richard to invite any woman alone to the flat? Either before he married or since?"

"Not to the flat. But I have heard Talk. I don't suppose it's anything to go on, and the woman who told my niece was one who'd talk about anything."

"What was the story, Mrs Tuck?"

"I don't like to repeat it, really. Only I suppose it doesn't matter now he's Gone. It was something about a woman out at Flogmore."

"Where's that?"

"It's a village about five miles away. Well, it *was* a village. I don't know what They'll do to it now. Turn it into another of these concentration camps like Maresfield, I dare say. But this wasn't in the village. This woman was supposed to be a gamekeeper's wife. Her husband had a cottage right in the woods, I believe."

"Do you know the name?"

"No. I only just heard the story. I might not have heard that, only my niece lives in Flogmore. She's married to a postman there. There may not be anything in it, but it won't hurt Richard repeating it now."

Carolus drank the last of his cowslip wine and prepared to depart.

"You be careful driving now," said Mrs Tuck. "If you have an accident They'll swear you was drunk and put you in prison for the rest of your life, and very likely me as well for giving it to you. They can't See In here, that's one thing, though I caught one at the window the other day. Said he'd come from the Health Department and was entitled to look before making his report. I tell you, They stop at nothing. So you go carefully."

"Thank you, Mrs Tuck. I always do. You've been most helpful."

She came to the door and pointed to a man down the road who carried a brief case.

"That's one of Them," she said. "He comes to inspect Mrs Rudd's little girl because someone told Them she slapped her for disobedience. They'll have her up, next."

Carolus made no comment as they drove away and Priggley was content to quote "'This other Eden, demi-Paradise'."

They were fortunate enough to find Mrs Romary at home. Her likeness to her brother Alan was at once apparent, but Carolus saw little in her dumpy and cheerful manner to suggest that she wished, as Pippa had said, to perpetuate her widowhood. She seemed even a little too cheerful for a member of a close-knit family which had been recently and dramatically bereaved.

"Alan said you would be coming to see me," she said. "I can't think how I can help you, but I'll certainly tell you anything I know."

"Thank you. May I just ask the formal questions first. Where were you on Saturday evening?"

"Here," said Mrs Romary promptly. "I did not go out at all."

"When did you last see Richard?"

"At Alan's on the afternoon before. We were playing tennis."

"Did you hear from him after that?"

"Yes. He rang me up on Saturday evening."

"Can you remember the time?"

"Not to the minute. I should say between eight-thirty and nine."

"Was it about anything important?"

"Not really. He often rang up for a chat."

"Did he say where he was?"

"He said he was at home. He was going to listen to a Beethoven Trio at 9.15."

"Perfectly calm?"

"You know, Mr Deene, when a thing like this happens one simply doesn't know how much one has imagined afterwards. I have a sort of feeling now that he wasn't at home because that would mean that almost certainly he was in bed. The phone's beside his bed and he liked lying there and chatting. He may have been, but as I remember it now he did not sound really relaxed."

"That's very interesting. But the impression was not strong enough to strike you at the time?"

"I suppose not. I dare say I've created it after hearing what has happened."

"Not necessarily. Now there's something else I have to ask you about. This, too, may be all imagination, though not mine. I have been told that your cousin . . . at least that there was talk about him and some woman out at Flogmore . . ."

Carolus was interrupted by Olivia Romary's rather loud laughter.

"What a place this is for scandal! Anything more absurd you could not imagine. I know exactly who you mean, but how such a story can have circulated I don't know. Were you told the name?"

"No. Only that she is a gamekeeper's wife."

"That's it! Florrie Lamplow. How ridiculous! We all knew Florrie and her husband, Tom Lamplow. Years ago, when Keith was quite a young boy, we took him out to Flogmore woods for a picnic and Tom Lamplow caught us trespassing. The shooting is hired by a syndicate which employed Tom, and he was just doing his job. But being a nice fellow and seeing that we were doing no harm he ended by joining us. You see, Mr Deene, whatever else my aunt is, she isn't a snob.

"After that it became a privilege of ours to picnic in the woods, and we often went to the Lamplows' cottage. Florrie was quite young then—well, she must be about thirty-three now. Rather a nice-looking woman. They were childless and she was devoted to Tom. They became friends of the family. They gave me my dog, a spaniel, when it was quite a pup. To suggest that there was anything between Richard and Florrie is simply malicious on someone's part."

"I quite believe that. *Pueblo chico, enfierno grande* is a Spanish proverb I've never found to fail."

107

" Meaning? "

" A small place, a big hell."

" You haven't heard the rest of the story. Poor Tom died, only about ten days ago, after an operation in the hospital here in Maresfield. Since then Florrie's been preparing to leave the cottage. We were awfully sorry for her. Only last Friday morning I motored out with Keith to see her and hear what she planned to do."

" You have a car, Mrs Romary? "

" Certainly. You don't think I'd be driven by Keith in that sports car of his. No thank you. His brother's just as bad a driver. Anita always insists on driving when they go out. We saw Florrie. She said she had to leave because the syndicate want the cottage for a new gamekeeper. She couldn't stay there alone, in any case; it's right out in the woods. No drainage or anything but rather pretty, like the gingerbread house. We found her packing-up. She was going back to Norfolk from which both she and Tom came. She said she wouldn't miss the people hereabouts because she had scarcely had anything to do with them, but she would miss her little house. It was thatched, you know, with latticed windows. Of course she missed Tom most of all. We tried to persuade her to stay in Maresfield, but there wasn't a hope. She had packed and was leaving ' any time now ' she said. She was a loyal soul and missed her husband dreadfully. You see how beastly it was of someone to suggest anything between her and Richard? "

" He may have met her in the town or given her a lift or something. It would be quite enough to start what Mrs Tuck calls ' Talk'."

" Oh, it was from Mrs Tuck you heard it? That explains it. That woman would say anything."

" On the contrary, Mrs Tuck didn't believe it. She told it me when I pressed her on a certain point, but only *as* Talk."

" Still, she told you."

" Whatever else Mrs Tuck may be I believe she is honest in her opinions," said Carolus.

" I'm sorry. I never liked or trusted her. And she could be abominably rude."

" That's sometimes an accomplishment," said Carolus smiling.

" I'm quite upset to hear there has been talk of Richard and Florrie, though. If you had known both of them you would understand, I'm sure. She gave me a present, by the way, when we were out last Friday. All very mysterious. ' Come up to my room because I've got something for you.' Keith wasn't even allowed to see it. It was an old sampler, lovely thing really. She didn't know who had done it, but she'd had it from her grandmother. Yes, we shall all miss Tom and Florrie."

Carolus stood up.

" Thank you for all you've told me," he said.

When they were in the car making for home Rupert asked why the family was ' so much against Mrs Tuck '.

" Because she's against them, I think. Don't you see, they are Them to her? All except Richard and Pippa."

12

KEITH came to lunch next day, arriving at the house in a sports car. He looked so young that Carolus was able to explain him to Mrs Stick as a friend of Rupert Priggley's.

" I'm depending on you for a mass of information," said Carolus. " I gather you knew Richard well."

" Yes, I did. And Pippa. I always liked her. She never seemed to mind my coming round and babbling with Richard. I did quite a lot of that, too. He was the only person in Maresfield who seemed to understand."

" What? "

" Well, me, I suppose."

" Are you another of these mixed-up kids, Keith? "

" Not really. Only I want to do things and I can never

understand what. I tried to paint some time ago and one or two people seemed to think I had something. But I don't know. Richard wanted me to take music seriously."

"You write, too?"

"No; that at least I know I can't do."

"I hear you have plans for starting a repertory theatre."

"Who told you that? It would be a good idea, you know. I don't believe television's got all *that* grip."

"What did Richard think about that?"

"He was interested."

"And your aunt?"

"I had not put it to her seriously. It was only an idea. But I could count on Richard to listen to whatever I was trying to do at the moment. So I did see quite a lot of him."

"During that last week?"

"Yes. He seemed perfectly all right. Rather cheerful, if anything. I think, you know, he always believed Pippa would come back to him."

"He seems to have been in some things unnaturally placid."

"Not exactly placid. Rather lazy. Fatalistic, you know. The last person one would expect to commit suicide. They say it *is* the last person one expects who does."

"Often, yes."

They were sitting in a little paved space outside the french windows and in the August heat the garden looked fulsomely bright. Mrs Stick came to know if they wanted drinks brought out.

"What will you have, Keith?"

"Gin, please. Lots of ice. Tonic, soda or whatever you have."

"Same for me," said Priggley, but Carolus told Mrs Stick to bring him a beer and a dry sherry for himself.

Carolus knew how to ask disturbing questions.

"Are you going to marry Wilma Day?" he said abruptly.

Keith reacted with all the violence one could expect. He spluttered over his drink and said, "Wilma Day?"

" Yes. Or doesn't your aunt approve? "

Keith forced a smile.

" You seem to have learned a great deal about us all,"
he said.

" And you want to know how much," said Carolus good-
humouredly. " Then let me tell you I know you intended
to spend that week-end with Wilma Day at the bungalow
at Marling Flats, that you were prevented from joining
her on Saturday by the arrival of Pippa at Lady Drumbone's, and on Sunday by the discovery of Richard Hoysden's body. That you finally went to fetch her on Monday
morning."

Keith looked blank.

" Did she tell you? "

" I have never met her."

" It's true, so far as it goes. Yes, I do want to marry
Wilma."

" And your aunt? "

" I just don't know. We've never dared let her guess.
She *doesn't* guess, does she? "

" Not that I know of. You must allow me to keep my
sources of information to myself."

" This is his favourite line," said Priggley. " I try to
make him see how corny it is, but nothing can be done."

" I shall have to tell her sooner or later, I suppose, about
Wilma and our plans for a repertory theatre . . ."

" Oh, Wilma's in that, too? "

" Very much. I want to direct it. I think that's what I
really could do, run a theatre. But Wilma's been keen
about it from the first. I'm not sure it wasn't her idea."

" I don't see why you should anticipate opposition from
your aunt, to either of your projects."

" Nor do I, really. It's just that I haven't had the guts
to tell her yet. She certainly won't like losing Wilma, who's
a first-rate secretary."

" Does it cost much to start a repertory theatre? "

" Well, we've got the place for it. There's a great barn
which somehow escaped the town planners. Magnificent it

is, one of the largest in the south of England. It would make a perfect theatre. The old idea—barn-stormers, you see. I've no use for all these amateur theatricals of Toffin's. I want the real thing. With a capital of five thousand pounds I believe we could start it."

"So why not?"

"Oh, we shall. Only this thing about Richard has upset everything. A suicide . . ."

Mrs Stick, coming out to announce lunch, caught the last word and gave Carolus what is rightly but too often called a withering look.

"Lunch is served," she said, and her words might have been 'the tumbrils are waiting'. She whispered something to Priggley.

"She'd like us to go in at once because it's a soufflay, she says."

Not the keenest hearing on Mrs Stick's part could detect during lunch a word which suggested that Keith was not a friend of Priggley's. Cricket was discussed, Wimbledon and Stirling Moss.

But when Mrs Stick had left the coffee on the table Carolus returned relentlessly to the matter in hand.

"Tell me," he said to Keith, " you knew Richard. What did you think when you heard he had shot himself? "

" I was shaken, of course. I never dreamt he had it in mind. Yet somehow I did not find it incredible. He was in some ways rather reserved. I mean, I was surprised, yes. but not so astounded as I might have been. But when I heard the recording then I really wouldn't believe it. Richard simply couldn't strangle a woman."

"There seems to be fairly general agreement on that point.'

"And anyway, they would know now, surely? They would have found her, whoever she was? For once my aunt was right, I believe. He imagined it."

"Let's put that aside for the moment, Keith, and stick to the recording. Richard says he killed someone whom he both hated and loved. He talked of her 'white on the green ground'. If he had even contemplated taking some-one that evening to a lonely place and strangling her, can you suggest where it might have been?"

"Yes, but it wasn't. The bungalow, I mean. Wilma was there at the time."

"Nowhere else?"

"I suppose there are thousands of places. I can't think of anywhere in particular. Unless . . ."

"Yes?"

"Do you think he might have gone to a place he knew well? Which we all knew well?"

"Possibly. Why?"

"Flogmore woods!" said Keith. "I don't know why I never thought of it before. We've been there scores of times for picnics. The keeper's a friend of ours, or was, poor chap. He died recently. If you're going to suppose the thing at all, that Richard was looking for a place in which to murder someone, that would be it."

"The wood's large?"

"Very. I forget how large. Several hundred acres, any-way. But he knew it well, as we all did. We had a number of favourite spots for picnics, and Richard could find his way to them in the dark."

"Just so. In the dark."

"Mind you, it still seems fantastic to me. But that would have been the place."

"It may have been," said Carolus grimly.

"You mean?"

"You should know better than I. Suppose your cousin murdered someone that evening, as he claims to have done, either in these woods or somewhere else. Suppose he took or simply left the body there. Could it have escaped discovery?"

"God! I see what you mean. So far as that's concerned it might not be found for a long time till a new keeper is appointed. Perhaps not even then if it was well hidden. But can you really suppose . . ."

"I'm pretty sure of one thing. We ought to take a look

at Flogmore woods and visit all the spots that were particularly known to Richard. Will you come, Keith? "

"Of course I'll come. I want to see Florrie Lamplow again, anyway. That's the keeper's wife. We've known her for ages and she's leaving one day soon if she hasn't already left. Going back to her home in Norfolk. You'll like her."

"That'll be a change," said Priggley. "Up to now this case of Carolus's has produced one of the ghastliest collections of women I remember. Except that redhead in the shop."

"Liz Gibbons, you mean? " said Keith smiling.

"I don't know her name. But what about Hipps? "

"Louise? She's always been a bit of a joke. Madly in love with Richard, I believe."

"And that drip Hilda in the Norfolk Hotel? "

"She hasn't much *joie de vivre*, I admit."

"I have not met your respected aunt, but I can't say I'm mad about your brother's wife."

"Anita tries to be a bit grand, but she's not a bad sort, really. What about Mrs Tuck, though? "

"Oh, I like Mrs Tuck," said Priggley.

"No one else does."

"I'm sure Rupert's prejudices are interesting," interrupted Carolus, "but there are one or two more points which I wanted to discuss with you, Keith. The pistol, for instance."

"It was Alan's. He's had it ever since the war."

"Did you all know that? "

"Yes. Last Christmas we spent at Mount Edgcumbe, Alan's house. My aunt generally throws the party, but Anita wanted to. After dinner . . ."

Priggley interrupted.

"*Not* amateur theatricals? "

"Worse. Charades. Alan got it out for something. He looked at it for about ten minutes to make sure it wasn't loaded, but even then Anita shrieked and told him to put it away at once, which he did."

"Who saw him lock it up? "

" All the men, I think. We were putting on absurd disguises up in his bedroom."

" Richard was there? "

" Yes."

" Who was at the party? "

" Only the family. My aunt, Alan, Anita, their two children, Richard and Pippa. Oh, Wilma was there, too. She couldn't go home for some reason and joined us."

" I see. Have you ever seen it again? "

" No."

" I gather there was a tennis-party there on Friday afternoon. Were the same men, more or less, in that bedroom? "

" Yes. But a character from the shop was there—Toffin. We used that bedroom and the women used Lucille's."

" *Not* Lucille? " sighed Priggley.

" The daughter, yes. She was away."

" And Richard would have had a chance to take the revolver? "

" I suppose so, yes. I believe he stayed upstairs for a shower when we went down for drinks. But he couldn't have been planning suicide that afternoon. He was enjoying himself enormously."

" I've said before in this case, the things suicides do are quite incomprehensible."

" You have. More than once," said Priggley. " What about this corpse hunt in the woods? "

Carolus apologized for this.

" Priggley's so anxious to appear blasé that he behaves like a child. Please forgive him."

Keith said: " Well, I don't take it much more seriously than that myself. I know it will be a waste of time."

Carolus seemed in no hurry to move, and lit a second cigar.

" By the way," asked Keith, " who was the last person to see Richard alive? "

" I don't know that," Carolus told him. " Quite possibly Wilma Day. You heard her evidence at the inquest, that he drove her to the station from Drumbone House."

"Yes, but surely . . . that was only seven-thirty. Don't we know anything of his movements after that?"

"Not really. He wasn't seen going in. He told the man upstairs, Hoskins, that he was going to listen to a Beethoven Trio which was coming on at nine-fifteen."

"I hope Wilma wasn't the last person to see him. I suppose someone could have gone to his flat without Slugley noticing?"

"Someone did, according to Slugley. A boy with sunglasses and a Grammar-School cap who had his arm in a sling."

Keith stared.

"*Charles?*" he said at last.

"It could scarcely have been anyone else. Slugley saw him going out by the service entrance soon after ten-thirty."

"But what on earth was Charles doing there?"

"I haven't asked him yet. I shall," said Carolus grimly. "He had some reason for seeing Richard, I gather. He owed money to the shop and wanted a saxophone on tick. He wasn't likely to get it while Toffin was around."

Keith smiled.

"No. Toffin's a bit of a watchdog. Pompous little man, but damned efficient."

"One other thing, Keith. Do you happen to know what your aunt was doing that evening?"

'No. We never know much of her movements."

"By her own account she didn't get back to her flat till ten forty-five."

"Might have been anywhere. A meeting or anything. She's a very busy woman."

"She must be. Does she drive her own car?"

"Oh, yes. Always. She likes that."

"Was she in to dinner?"

"We don't really have dinner at night. There are two women who work for my aunt, Mrs Runciman and her sister Kate. Middle-aged. Been with her some time. They do the lunch and leave something cold in the Frigidaire, usually. If my aunt and I and Wilma are alone, as we often are, Wilma usually puts it on the table about seven. That evening she was rushing off, as you know, and I got it ready. It was just a cold roast chicken and salad. We had it soon after Wilma had left. My aunt asked her to eat something before she went, but she hadn't time. I don't think we were at the table more than twenty minutes, and soon after that my aunt went out."

"Without saying where she was going?"

"If she did I don't remember. I think she called out 'I shan't be late'."

"And she has said nothing since?"

"No. Why don't you ask her?" said Keith.

"Your aunt is expert at asking questions, but doesn't much like answering them."

"I see what you mean."

"Now, do we go?" suggested Priggley.

They stood up.

"I warn you it's a waste of time from your point of view," Keith said.

"I'd like to see these woods, anyway. I'm surprised they've been left standing so long."

"I believe there's a plan to build there now."

"There's always a plan," said Carolus.

13

IT was decided that Keith's car should be left outside the house while they went and returned in Carolus's Bentley. They passed through Maresfield at five o'clock, and not many minutes later, it seemed, they came to Flogmore village.

"This has been left pretty well alone," remarked Carolus, seeing the carelessly grouped old cottages and houses round a church.

"They're just going to start on it," said Keith. "I read

an article in the county paper last week. It has so far been categorized as an area of 'high landscape value'. But with the 'proliferation of households' . . ."

" What? "

" At a rate unforeseen by the planners, such unprotected values must go by the board. The 'rate of occupancy' in this region has dropped from 3·3 persons to a dwelling to 2·7, it seems. In-filling . . ."

"Oh, for God's sake," said Priggley.

" At any rate, Flogmore is scheduled as a semi-rural residential area and the woods we are about to go through will disappear before this time next year."

They drove on by a narrow road between overgrown rhododendrons.

"Take the next to the left," said Keith. "It's only a cart-track, so you'll have to take it easy. All right at this time of year, but tricky in winter. I don't know how Tom and Florrie managed—they came into the village on bicycles."

Carolus turned with some difficulty into a sort of enlarged rabbit-run which had branches that met over it. He continued for a hundred yards, then the track had a sharp right bend. The keeper's cottage, when it came in sight, he reckoned to be two hundred yards from the road.

They pulled up in a clearing. There was an extraordinary, an almost unnatural, peace there. It was not silent, for the wood-pigeons coo'd continuously and there was audible a buzzing undertone of insects. But no dog barked, no human being appeared, and when the engine of the car was switched off it left only a sleepy hum about them.

The soft afternoon light was on the cottage. It had been constructed about a century before, the sort of mock-gothic thing that estate owners built for their lodge-keepers and gardeners, but because it was thatched and had latticed windows and hollyhocks in the front garden it had the prettiness of a coloured postcard, a sentimental, pseudo-romantic prettiness which its position among the trees emphasized. The windows were closed and no smoke came from the chimney.

Keith went up to the front door and knocked, but he did not wait long.

"I *thought* Florrie might have gone," he said. "It's a pity, because I should have liked you to meet her."

They peered through the diamond panes of the windows, and at first could see nothing of the dark interior. But as their eyes grew used to it they could make out several tea-chests and general preparations for the removal of the furniture. They walked to the back of the house and found an empty fowl-run and two untenanted kennels.

"It seems an awful shame," said Keith. "Tom wasn't old, you know, and they were awfully happy together. I first came to this cottage when I was quite a kid, and I don't know how often since."

When they reached the front of the cottage again a post-man was approaching on a bicycle. He was a fat young man who seemed to be feeling the heat.

"She's gone," he said, rather superfluously.

"Do you know when?"

"Week-end, it must have been. She wasn't here on Monday morning. But she never came to the post office to say, and that means I have to come right out here whenever there's a letter."

"Are there many?"

"No. This is the first since Monday's. I put that in the box. Pity about Tom, wasn't it? He was a good chap."

"Will there be another game-keeper?" asked Carolus.

"Shouldn't think so. They say they're going to build all over here. Next year they're supposed to be starting. This'll be the last season's shooting, I reckon. Are you from the syndicate?"

"No," said Keith. "We're friends of Mrs Lamplow's. We didn't know she had already left."

"Yes, been gone some days. She sold all her livestock last week. Oh, well, I must be getting on."

He walked up to the front door, shoved a letter through the slot and, climbing carefully to the seat of his cycle, rode away.

"Now," said Priggley, "what about our walk through the woods?"

"I'll take you by the path which Tom used to call his beat. The wood is, roughly speaking, a rectangle, and this path, though it winds a good deal, makes an irregular oval within it. At one or two points it comes right out of the trees, but for the most part it keeps between them. You would have to know the way into it to follow it. Rather like a maze."

But before they entered the wood Keith called them to an outhouse at the back.

"Have a look at this," he said.

There in rather dim light they saw an extraordinary piece of mechanism. It was long disused and covered with rust, but its shape could still be seen, like a huge set of artificial teeth made of iron.

"It's a man-trap," said Keith. "Tom said they've been illegal for more than a century, but it could still be made to work. Look at those teeth! They snap right through a man's shin bone. In the old days when they were set up in the woods hidden by leaves no one could ever escape from them if they once closed. Tom said his father knew an old man who was caught in one as a boy and was lamed for life."

Carolus examined the thing.

"You say it could still be made to work?"

"Tom said so. All it wants is a drop of oil, he told me, and it would be as good as new. But no one would dare set it now."

"I suppose not. Let's go on."

From the cultivated patch behind the house Keith turned sharp right and in a moment entered the wood at a point known to him. It seemed that Tom had kept his beat clear of overgrowth, for they were able to progress in a single file without much difficulty.

"I feel more Fenimore Cooper than Conan Doyle," said Priggley. "How long do we play Indians on the war-path?"

"Tom's beat must be well over a mile long with all its windings."

They left the smaller bushes and came suddenly to the cool shade of tall beeches with great smooth trunks with little pools of brackish water beneath them. Here it was possible to look ahead for some distance, and the path they were following was no longer easily seen.

"You have to know the way here," said Keith. "When I first came I used to mark certain trees, but it soon became unnecessary."

They came to a fallen tree-trunk.

"This was one of our favourite spots," said Keith.

It was certainly cool and peaceful. The ground was littered with old beechnut husks, but there was no sign of disturbance here. The dark green moss looked untrodden.

They pushed on for a time, entering a thicker wood in which their progress was slower, and once or twice brambles had grown across the path since Tom Lamplow had been here to clear it.

Suddenly Carolus became aware of a smell of putrefaction, and stopped. There was no mistaking that stench—rotting flesh. But Keith smiled.

"It's all right," he said. "Not what you think. Come on and I'll show you."

They came in a moment on the keeper's gibbet, a line stretched from tree to tree on which Tom Lamplow had hung the corpses of his enemies, rats, weasels, a stoat or two, hawks, several magpies, two jays and one crow.

"Some keepers shoot owls," remarked Keith, "but Tom didn't believe in it. I think he'd rather have shot poachers."

A few minutes later Keith said, "This is the point about farthest from the house. We start returning now."

"Glad you told me," said Rupert. "I've lost all sense of direction."

They came to another clearing, a particularly inviting place in which were some great stones, roughly oblong in shape.

" This was where Tom found us picnicking the first day. We had come in from the far side of the wood. A road runs there. These stones made good seats. They're supposed to have been used for building once. No doubt an archæologist would know all about them—we just sat on them."

This place, too, seemed undisturbed. But here they rested for a time and smoked.

Another walk of ten minutes brought them, Keith said, quite near the keeper's house, though they could not see it.

" This is our last haunt," he said. " It's an artificial clearing, as you see."

It was, in fact, a complete circle. Everything had been cleared from it, but the bright grass which grows under trees. It suggested woodland scenes of literature, or perhaps of mythology.

" Don't start talking about fairies," begged Rupert, then suddenly asked sharply—" What's that? "

' That ' was something white a few yards away.

Long before they reached it they guessed what they would find, for this time the stench was unmistakable. It was the body of a woman in a horrid state of recent decay. She wore only an old-fashioned white night-gown, and she lay on her back.

" God," said Keith. " It's Florrie."

He was about to stoop down when Carolus said, " No. Touch nothing."

He examined the ground closely, but after staring down at the face for a moment or two he kept away from the corpse itself.

" How far are we from the cottage? "

" Not twenty yards," said Keith, who looked very white. " You'll see. Can't we . . . can't we do something? She mustn't be left like that! "

" It won't be for long."

" Can't we at least cover her? "

" We'll phone the police," said Carolus. " This is their job. She's been strangled, I think."

In a moment they came out of the cover of the trees to the clearing in which the keeper's house stood.

"I want to look inside," said Carolus.

"Hell, can't you do that later? I feel . . ." Keith looked ghastly.

"Sit down a minute," said Carolus. "I know it's rotten for you. But there's something I must know."

Rupert tried every ground-floor window, but they were closed and both doors were locked.

"Can you climb up to that window? It's open."

The window was at the back of the house, and Rupert pulled himself to the roof of what appeared to be an outside lavatory. From this he reached the ledge and hauled himself up.

"Don't open anything," ordered Carolus. "And don't touch anything. Just look at the beds."

Rupert disappeared, but in a few moments returned to the window.

"There's only one," he said. "A double bed. It has been slept in and not made up."

"That's all I want to know."

Rupert climbed down again and they went to the car.

"Better stop in the village," he said. "You need some brandy, Keith. I could do with a drink myself."

"You were right, damn you," said Keith a little hysterically. "You were determined to find a corpse and you have. Poor Florrie. She never hurt anyone. Why *her*, of all people?"

"Pull yourself together," said Carolus.

"Sorry," said Keith. "It isn't just . . . death. It was . . . you saw the state she was in. How long do you think she has been there?"

"Some days, anyhow. Here's the pub. Come along in. Say nothing here, of course. I shan't phone from here, I think. We'll be back in Maresfield in a few minutes."

Keith recovered quickly, but said little on the way to Maresfield. Priggley suggested that if Keith did not want to come over to Carolus's home at Newminster, he,

Priggley, would be delighted to bring Keith's sports car in the morning. Keith accepted this offer and Carolus dropped him at Drumbone House.

Priggley remained in the car while Carolus entered the police station and asked at the desk for Detective Inspector Bowler. He was taken to a small office where he met the wiry, intelligent-looking plain-clothes man whom John Moore had described as a 'good chap'.

Bowler offered Carolus a chair, but seemed determined to let him take the lead in any conversation there was to be.

"I understand from John Moore who is a friend of mine that you resent my investigating in this case," said Carolus.

"I didn't say that, exactly," replied Bowler, but made no effort to explain what he did say.

"You're convinced that it is a straightforward suicide?"

"I could not possibly discuss it."

"Even if I have some information for you?"

Bowler remained quite unruffled and courteous, but equally firm.

"If you have any information relating to this or any other matter which you know the police require, Mr Deene, it's your duty to report it. You know that as well as I do."

"Yes. I'm going to report it. But I can't help wanting to know—it's only human—whether you believe Richard Hoysden killed someone or not? You've heard the tape-recording."

"I'm prepared to go so far as to admit there are some very puzzling features in this case."

"That's handsome of you," said Carolus. "There's that 'Oh, hell!' for instance."

Did Bowler nod? Or shake his head? Or remain perfectly still? Carolus could not decide.

"Then there's the pistol."

"Yes," assented Bowler cannily.

"And the schoolboy with his arm in a sling."

The most concentrated scrutiny did not reveal to Carolus whether or not he was giving the policeman news.

"There's that, too," assented Bowler.

For a mischievous minute he wondered whether to invent a touch of fantasy and say, for instance, 'there's Miss Hipps's feather boa', or 'there's the matter of that armadillo', to see whether Bowler would gravely assent. Instead he said, "And now I've got something to add to these."

Bowler looked up, but Carolus was determined to make him ask a question. After a silent thirty seconds, he did.

"What's that?"

"Another body," returned Carolus.

"I hope," said Bowler, "you are not trying to be funny, Mr Deene."

"No."

"What kind of body?"

"Very, very nauseous. Dead some days in this hot weather."

"I mean male or female?"

Carolus, in spite of the somewhat macabre catechism, began to enjoy himself.

"I did not make any minute inspection, but I think I can safely say female."

"Do you know whose body it is?"

"No. Who *does* own a dead body?"

"I mean who it was?"

"Yes. It was the wife of a game-keeper called Lamplow."

"Where is it?"

"In Flogmore woods."

"And how did you come to stumble on it, Mr Deene?"

"Fortunately I didn't stumble on it. It is quite untouched. I found it by doing the normal common-sense thing in the circumstances—looking in the places where Richard Hoysden was likely to have left a body."

"I see. And Flogmore woods was the normal common-sense place?"

"It was. You see I was never so convinced as you that this was a straightforward suicide with no strings attached. Talking about strings, I think this woman was strangled."

"Oh, you do. What makes you say that?"

"I'm not sure. The decomposition was considerable and I made no detailed examination. But the neck and the face suggested it. There was no 'silk cord no more than a yard long' though."

"When did you make this discovery, Mr Deene?"

"About forty minutes ago."

Bowler further wanted to know, who had been with Carolus, who had been told of the discovery, and whether Carolus had taken any steps to see that the body was not touched in the meantime. In answer to the last Carolus said rather huffily that it had obviously lain for a good many days and there seemed no reason why it should be moved now.

"Do you happen to know whether the dead woman was known to Richard Hoysden?" asked Bowler.

"Yes. She was."

"Intimately?"

"His housekeeper, Mrs Tuck, informs me that though I should not take any notice of it there had been 'talk' about them."

"I see. I suppose I ought to thank you, Mr Deene. You discovered this before I did."

"I was informed of the recording before you," said Carolus consolingly.

"Now, would you be kind enough to accompany me to the place where you made this discovery?"

"No. I draw the line at that. I'm going to the Norfolk for a drink. But I have in my car outside someone eminently suitable to guide you. A pupil of mine with such ghoulish tastes that another sight of the corpse will positively cheer him."

"I see."

"Besides, it will be some time before you can start. You have to get a photographer and whatnot. Priggley will take you to the spot. I'll tell him to join me at the Norfolk when you bring him back."

"Very well."

"I take it you won't be too long because the light will soon be fading?"

"No."

"It's not pleasant, I assure you."

"They seldom are," said Bowler, and picked up the telephone.

Carolus sent Priggley into the CID office and made for the Norfolk Hotel.

14

HE found Hilda wilting behind her bar.

"Good evening," he said brightly.

"You were in the other day, weren't you? I thought you were, though I can't be bothered to notice most that come in. They make me tired."

"Yes. I see that," said Carolus ambiguously.

"It isn't as though they'd got anything to say, most of them."

"Perhaps you don't encourage them much?"

"Well, I've not a lot of time for them, I must admit. I suppose some of them's all right in their own way, but you can't really feel interested, can you?"

"Yes," said Carolus. "Has Mr Alan Bourne been in? The cousin of the man who committed suicide?"

"Is that what he is? I didn't know," said Hilda indifferently. "Yes, he was in last night. Seemed to be drinking rather a lot, but it's no business of mine. I don't care for anyone like that."

"Was he alone?"

"He was when he came in, but later he was talking to a man called Toffin, I believe. I didn't take much notice, to tell the truth. Well, you don't, do you?"

"Yes," said Carolus. "Does anyone come in here from Flogmore?"

"I believe Mr Rothsay, who stays here quite a bit, is one of those who go shooting out there. I seem to remember him talking about it, though I've not a lot of use for shooting things. He's here now, as a matter of fact."

"Where?"

"In the hotel, I mean. He's having his dinner at the moment, I expect. He will be in presently."

"Would you mind pointing him out to me when he comes in?"

"If I remember, I will. Though I'd rather you picked him out for yourself. I don't like getting mixed up in anything like that. You'll know him. Wears a check suit and a buttonhole. A moustache. Rather a sporty type, I suppose, though I don't know much about that sort. I'm sure you'd recognize him, though. There won't be all that number in tonight, I don't expect. It isn't often there is."

The first customer to enter, however, was not Rothsay, but the tall and taciturn Mr Hoskins. He had certainly chosen the right bar, thought Carolus.

"Pint," he said to Hilda, with a nod, thus combining in this monosyllable his greeting and order.

But Carolus felt the man's attention was on him, and that within that sullen frame a volcano of loquacity was preparing to erupt. He was not mistaken. Mr Hoskins approached him with a nod of recognition and spoke five words.

"Wanted to speak to you," he explained with a painful effort.

"Yes?"

"I told you I didn't go down to Hoysden's flat. I did."

"What time?"

"Just after eight."

"And he was in?"

"Just got back."

"Where from? Do you know?"

"Didn't say."

"Did you stay long?"

"Few minutes."

" Why are you telling me this now? "

That, it was clear, was asking Mr Hoskins to go too far. It would take at least a dozen words to explain, whether it was that he disliked inaccuracy, feared that Carolus would hear from someone else, or had previously lied on an impulse which he regretted. Nor did Carolus press his question.

" Did you go for any particular reason? "

Mr Hoskins shook his head.

" Just for a few minutes' chat? "

" Ay," said Mr Hoskins, and seemed to feel better for emitting his favourite sound at last. Having done so, he picked up the remaining two-thirds of his pint of bitter and swallowed it with no sign of enjoyment.

" Night," he said and was gone.

" He's not very talkative, is he? " said Carolus apologetically to Hilda.

" I can't see why you bother with him, really. It's muggy tonight, isn't it? Tiring weather, really. I feel as though I'd been on my feet all day."

" And haven't you? "

Just then a man entered whom, as Hilda had predicted, Carolus identified at once as Rothsay. The large carnation backed by a piece of asparagus fern, the face which appeared, whether by nature or design, stupid, the brilliant black and white of the suit-pattern, the florid moustache: Rothsay lacked only a bowler hat and a pair of field glasses.

Carolus was feeling thankful for Hilda's lethargy and unwillingness to ' get mixed up ' when she unfortunately addressed him.

" This is the gentleman you were asking about," she said loudly. " This gentleman was asking for you, Mr Rothsay," she added as though to make quite sure that everyone understood everyone else. She then retired into sulky indifference.

Rothsay eyed Carolus suspiciously as though he expected to be offered a good thing for Epsom.

" Want me? " he asked cagily.

" Yes," said Carolus. Then, on an inspiration, he decided to put the cart before the horse. " You're one of the syndicate which employed Tom Lamplow as a gamekeeper, aren't you? "

Rothsay answered this sharply and defensively.

" The widow has been looked after," he said, still convinced that Carolus meant to touch him for something.

" You're very right," said Carolus. " I found her body this afternoon. She was murdered about a week ago."

Mr Rothsay goggled in a highly satisfactory way, but Hilda, who was listening, did not seem pleased.

" I don't care for anything like that, I must say," she said with something more like animation than her customary whine.

" Murdered? " repeated Rothsay as though he had not heard.

" Strangled, I think. The police will know all about that."

Rothsay began to collect himself.

" You're not the police? "

" No. I'm investigating Richard Hoysden's death for Lady Drumbone."

Rothsay, like a boxer who has scarcely risen to his feet, went down again.

" But what's that to do with what you've just told me? "

" Quite a lot, I should guess. Wouldn't you? "

" Scarcely up my street," said Rothsay, now on his feet once more.

" I was hoping you might be able to help me. You seem to be one of the few people outside the family having connections with *both* affairs."

" Me? Both? I see what you mean. Scarcely connections."

Rothsay was tottering.

" I wouldn't know. But you've been living with Richard Hoysden's wife and you employed the husband of the woman who caused him to be talked about, the woman who is now dead."

Rothsay clung to the ropes.

"Scarcely 'living with', old man. Pippa came up to town with me. Little change. Less than a fortnight."

"Change of what? Air?"

"She needed it. This family got her down."

"I'm not surprised from what I've seen of them," put in Hilda, the corners of her mouth almost meeting in the middle of her chin. "They get me down. I know that."

"And you think Richard Hoysden thought of it like that?" persisted Carolus.

"Sure of it, old man. Know he did."

"Why? Did you ask him?"

"Not in so many words. But I knew his character. Just how he'd look at it. Bit of a change for Pippa."

"You didn't, for instance, go to see him that evening?"

"Which evening, old man?"

"The evening you brought Pippa back to Marcsfield. The evening Richard shot himself. Last Saturday, in fact."

"Go and see him? Whatever gives you that idea? It would be the last thing in the circumstances."

"Did you?"

"Certainly not. Scarcely knew him."

"You knew him well enough to be sure about his attitude to his wife's disappearance."

"Different thing." Rothsay was on his feet and sparring now. "Instinct. Certainly couldn't have gone to see him."

"Then what . . ." Carolus held his straight left for a moment then let it go clean to the solar plexus, "then what was your car doing in the parking place of his building?"

One, two, three, four, five, six, seven . . .

"What?"

Carolus did not answer.

"What do you mean, old man? My car? The Mercedes? In the parking place? Which parking place?"

"Behind the block of flats over Richard's music shop," said Carolus patiently but clearly.

"When was this?"

"About ten o'clock."

"Nonsense. Can't have been. Must have been another Mercedes."

Carolus watched these struggles, as though waiting for the referee to stand back. He said nothing.

"Unless I popped in the building to see someone else," tried Rothsay.

"No," said Carolus firmly.

"Or left it there while I was at the pictures."

"What pictures?"

"The pictures, old man. Cinema." Rothsay was gamely recovering his balance.

"There isn't a cinema anywhere near there. And both the town cinemas have their own car parks."

"Then it must have been another Mercedes. I've been told there's another in the town. You've heard that, haven't you, Hilda?"

"Oh, I don't know anything about it. I don't want to know either. Not when it comes to it."

"Did you know Florrie Lamplow?" Carolus asked Rothsay.

Rothsay appeared relieved but still wary.

"The keeper's wife, you mean? Just to speak to. She gave me a cup of tea once. Nice little cottage. Pity they're going to build."

"When did you see her last?"

"Who? Florrie Lamplow? Oh, ages ago. Last winter."

"Ever heard Richard speak of her?"

"No. Can't say I did. He seemed to talk of nothing but music. That's what bored Pippa."

"It would me, too," said Hilda. "If there's one thing I can't seem to take to it's a lot of music."

Rothsay was fighting back now.

"You ask a hell of a lot of questions, old man," he said. "I can't see what I've got to do with it."

Carolus was preparing a right hook.

"What did you do last Saturday evening, Rothsay? After you'd dropped Pippa here?"

"Me? Last Saturday?" This time he was no more than momentarily groggy. "Drove back to town."

"Yes, I know. But I meant immediately after you had dropped Pippa."

"Had one or two."

"Where?"

"Oh, on the way. Here and there. Nowhere special. I don't think we'll have any more questions, old man. Had about enough. It's nothing to do with me. And quite frankly, I can't see what it's to do with you."

"Just as you like."

In spite of Rothsay's bravado, Carolus could see the man staring at him as though wondering where the next blow would strike him. He soon discovered.

"You've told me what I wanted to know," said Carolus.

"What do you mean? What did you want to know? What have I told you?"

"I thought we were to have no more questions."

"That's a very peculiar thing to say, though. Told you what you want to know. I can't see that I've told you anything. Besides, I've got nothing to tell. Not my line of country. Nasty business."

"Very," assented Carolus.

"I mean to say, even the police haven't asked me anything."

"They only heard of Mrs Lamplow's death an hour ago. They have plenty of time."

"Extraordinary business. Anyway, have a drink?"

"No, thanks."

"Not a drink? Why not?"

"No, thank you."

"I hope you've got no reason for refusing a drink with me?"

"I hope that, too."

"I don't like it, old man. You ask me a whole lot of questions about these deaths then refuse a drink with me."

Carolus did not answer.

" Will *you* have a drink? " Rothsay asked Hilda.

" It's rather early, but I'll make an exception," she conceded, pouring herself a gin-and-tonic.

" Anyway," said Rothsay to Carolus, " *she* doesn't think I strangled a game-keeper's wife."

He paid for the drink and left.

" It's only half-past eight," said Hilda. " The evenings seem to get longer and longer. Sometimes I think I shall never get through to closing-time."

" Why don't you read a book? " asked Carolus.

" I'm not all that fond of reading," explained Hilda. " Well, it's a waste of time really, isn't it? "

" No," said Carolus, and turned to see, greatly to his surprise, Keith Bourne come in with Wilma Day.

Keith also seemed surprised.

" I don't think you've met," he said, and introduced Wilma and Carolus.

" I've heard a lot about you," the girl smiled. Priggley had been right—she was extremely pretty.

" I've just been telling Wilma about our shock this afternoon."

" It must have been frightful for you all," sympathized the girl.

" It was frightful for me," said Keith, " because I knew Florrie. But Mr Deene took it very calmly. I suppose the police have been out there? "

" They are there now."

" Did you know the dead woman, Miss Day? " Carolus asked quietly.

" I met her once when we all went out there. She seemed an awfully nice kind sort of person."

" She was," said Keith.

It was evident to Carolus that these two were very much in love. Not from any gesture or sign of endearment, not even from looks exchanged or tone of voice, though it was implicit in all these. To use a rather grand word, Carolus thought, there was an aura about them. One knew that the comradeship they showed was merely external and that inwardly they were securely bound by ties which neither wanted to break. Their faces looked very young contrasted with the drooping and dissatisfied features of Hilda, and as usual with any young couple deeply in love they had a sort of pathos.

" Let me buy you a drink," said Keith. " No, you bought me a brandy this evening and it saved my life. What is it? Whisky? And what are you having, darling? "

Wilma asked for port.

" Will you have one? " Keith asked Hilda.

" It's rather early," said Carolus, " but she'll make an exception. Won't you? "

Could that curious fluttering at the mouth-tips be a smile?

Priggley joined them a few minutes later and said that the remains of Florrie Lamplow had been taken to the mortuary.

" I shouldn't like that," mentioned Hilda.

But Carolus was watching the faces of the two young lovers. It was clear that nothing that happened except to themselves could do much to disturb them.

15

NEXT morning Carolus hesitated not at all in Maresfield, but drove out to Flogmore woods. He was alone today, for Priggley had excused himself on the grounds that he wanted to swim and was going down to the coast on his motor-cycle. Carolus found the point where the track to the game-keeper's cottage left the lane, and was about to turn when he saw a woman hurrying from a cottage which overlooked the entrance to the track. She had, it seemed, been putting out her laundry when she saw the car, for she still held in her hand a pair of pink knickers, though she was evidently far too excited to be aware of the garment. She was blonde and sinewy, and shouted " Just a minute! " as she approached.

Carolus pulled into the side of the road and waited for her to come breathlessly to the car windows.

" Are you from the newspapers? " she asked.

" Yes," lied Carolus without hesitation.

" Come about the murder? "

" Yes."

" Got your camera with you? "

" No. I shall send a photographer out later if there's a story."

" Oh, yes! There's a story! " panted the woman. " Wait till you hear what I can tell you! "

" I should very much like to."

" You better come inside then. I don't want everyone else to know my business."

" Don't you? Then . . ."

" Oh, I mean neighbours and that. Let them read it in the papers if they want to, not come eavesdropping to what I'm going to tell you."

Carolus followed the woman to a small front room of her cottage and found himself wedged between an upright piano and a flowerpot stand. The woman faced him exultantly.

" Would you like to ask the questions or shall I just tell you all I know? " she asked.

Carolus then made a grave tactical error.

" You just tell me," he said, and a moment later realized his blunder.

" My name's Redlove, Daisy Redlove. R-e-d-l-o-v-e. My husband's a farm foreman, Herbert Redlove. Aren't you going to write that down? "

Carolus, beginning to see his mistake, produced paper and pencil and began doodling industriously in a pattern which he hoped resembled shorthand.

" I've been married twelve years," went on Mrs Redlove, " but we've only just the two children Arthur and Margaret. They're at school now. Here's a photo of them taken at Westgate last summer. I can't let you take that away with you, I'm afraid. It's the only one I've got. Tell you what, though, I've got an extra one of me and my husband coming out of the church when we were married, so you can have that. Better write on the back of it, 'Parish Church, Flogmore, June 7th, 1949.' Well, as I was saying, we've lived in this cottage ever since we were married, and although it's cold in the winter we've got used to it now and the children have never known anything else."

"About the Lamplows," interrupted Carolus.

"I'm just coming to them. Well, they were here before we were, so you'd have thought being their nearest neighbours we should have found them friendly, but they seemed to want to keep to themselves, so in all these years I haven't worried about them. I soon had the children to think of, and the older one, that's the little girl, had such a passion for music that nothing would satisfy her till we had her taught the piano. That's some of her music beside you there. She can play all that. It's wonderful, really, because she's only eleven. I suppose you could take a picture of her sitting at the piano, here, couldn't you? It doesn't seem to matter about the light for pictures now because you see them taken of Princess Margaret coming out of the theatre at night. Only I should like to know what time you'll be coming, because I want to see she's dressed nice for it."

"Yes. Mrs Lamplow was . . ."

"Well, as I was saying, we moved in after them, and the first time I met her in the street I thought it was only right to tell her who we were. I must say she was quite polite, but she didn't say anything like where she lived if we needed anything, as anyone would. I thought to myself, you're not very friendly to anyone just moving in, but I didn't say it.

"*He* was just the same. He used to go into the Woodmen's in the evening sometimes where my husband won the darts championship. There was a bit in the paper about that, then later a photo of him with all the other cham-

137

pions from all over the country. I think I've got a copy of that you could have. Yes, there he is at the back. That's my husband with the cup in his hand. Well, they've all got cups, but that's him in the corner . . ."

"Lamplows."

"Well, as I was saying, when I was expecting the little girl I *did* think this Mrs Lamplow would say something, but I saw her go by on her bicycle many a time without stopping. It was the same with others in the village, she never seemed to mind whether she knew you or didn't. She only had the one friend, that was Mrs Beale at the shop, and they were very thick. What are you writing that down for? Mrs Beale won't have a lot to tell you; she'll be too Upset. Still, you know what you're doing. No sooner had I had the little girl, it seemed, before I was expecting again and the little boy was born within the year of the girl. He was a bonny baby. Well, everyone said so. I've got a picture of him somewhere which I often thought of sending up to one of the papers. I've been told more than once it would win a competition."

"Lamplows," insisted Carolus feebly.

"Of course, *he* went very sudden. You could put that bit in: 'Mrs Redlove says dead woman's husband died very sudden.' I never really knew what it was; he seemed to be all right one day and taken to hospital the next, and before we knew where we were we heard he was dead. Something to do with the liver, they say. And he was a big, strong-looking chap, and no age really. It makes you Think, when they're Taken like that. Same as my sister Went. She lived in the village here because her husband worked at the nurseries in Maresfield. She went just as sudden. Only it was kidneys with her, the doctor said. But she had a beautiful funeral. I can show you a picture somewhere, only I don't suppose you'd need that, would you? Not with all the others you'll have. You should have seen the flowers! One of the undertaker's men told me he'd never seen so many flowers at one time. So it shows, doesn't it? "

"Lamp . . ."

"Well, as I was saying, when he'd Gone we heard she was moving away. Young Roger Goode, the postman, was about the only one who used to go up to their cottage. She used to take her milk back herself and there was no call for anyone to go out all that way. I don't think young Roger knew much of them, but he used to see her when there was letters for her. It was him told me she was going, after Tom Lamplow died. 'She's packing everything up,' he said, 'so I suppose she's leaving.' Some said they wanted the cottage for another game-keeper, and then again that it wouldn't be worth while because this is all going to be built over next year. I suppose that means our cottage which is more than a hundred years old will be pulled down. You better write this part down, that we say we won't live in a council house. 'Herbert and Daisy Redlove, who came to their cottage straight from the church they was married in, say they won't live in council house.' Then you could put it with a picture of us standing in front, with the dog in with us if he'd keep still."

"Lamplows," persisted Carolus, less gently.

"Well, as I was saying, I knew she was going, but I never imagined she'd go off in the middle of the night like that. At least that's what we thought. We weren't to know the poor woman had been strangled and lying out there all this time, were we? So when I heard this car . . ."

"Which car?"

"That's what I'm saying. I heard it because I'm a light sleeper. Not like my husband. Nothing will wake him up once he's got off. He didn't know anything about it till the morning when I told him Mrs Lamplow had gone off in the night, as I thought."

"Which night was that, Mrs Redlove?"

"That's right. You write this down. 'Mrs Redlove of Brook Cottage, Flogmore, hears Murder Car.' It was the Saturday night, I heard it. Well, the Sunday morning, really, because it was past two o'clock. I thought to myself, I wonder why she's flitting off like that, because from all accounts she didn't owe a penny and there was the furniture, too."

"You say you heard a car drive up soon after two o'clock?"

"That's when it came, yes, because I struck a match and looked at the clock. Then it drove away again."

"How long afterwards?"

"Must have been at least an hour. I can't be sure of that because I'd dozed off, but you can tell. Anyhow we know now, don't we? Because he must have done for her in that time while he was up there and then made off again. You write that down. 'Mrs Redlove says murderer was at death house for an hour. Farmer's wife a light sleeper.' Well, you can call my husband a farmer, being a farm foreman, can't you? Only you want a good picture when you take it. I think you should have Arthur and Margaret in too, because they might remember something and they was ever so excited when they heard about it before they went off to school this morning. You know what children are when anything out of the way happens, and there's not much going on about here till they begin building. We haven't got the telly yet, so it's something for them to say to the other kids who always start talking about the shooting and that they've seen on the telly the night before. Is there anything else you want to know about?"

"Yes. Have you any idea what kind of car it was? Did it sound like a large car?"

"Not like a lorry, it didn't, but it wasn't a bubble car or anything like that. Just an ordinary car I should say. Of course I didn't see it, but you can tell pretty well. Write that down, I should. 'Mrs Redlove says murder car not a lorry.'"

Carolus doodled industriously.

"Is that all then? There's that £50 we won in the pools two years ago if that . . ."

"Had the Lamplows many visitors?"

"You'd be surprised. There was often someone popping

out to see them and I've wondered more than once who they were. Nice cars, you know, and up there for a long time. At first I thought it was all part of the shooting, but they seemed to come more in the summer than winter."

"You didn't know any of them?"

"No, I can't say I did, not to recognize them," said Mrs Redlove regretfully. "You could just put that Mrs Redlove said there were frequent visitors in cars at the death house before the night of the murder. That would do, wouldn't it?"

"Do you remember a car coming out on the Friday morning?"

"Well, I can't say I do, really. Of course there were lots of cars only I wouldn't have noticed before this happened, and I don't really know one from another. Is that an important part, because I could ask my husband only I doubt if he'd know any better than what I would."

Carolus thanked Mrs Redlove and prepared to leave.

"What would be the best for me to wear when you bring your photographer? I've got the dress I go to the dances in. It's a sort of bluey emerald colour . . ."

"That would be excellent," said Carolus, now past the piano and the plant pot and on his way through the door.

"What about my husband?" asked Mrs Redlove following him.

"Black. Certainly black," said Carolus absently as he opened the front gate.

"He's got his blue serge," said Mrs Redlove, "if you think that would do? And I've just bought a new dress for Margaret so we shall be all right."

Carolus achieved his driving-seat and started the engine.

"You could say how sorry I was about it, too, because she was a next-door neighbour, really. 'I have lost a friend', says Mrs Redlove, of Brook Cottage, Flogmore. Only then I think I ought to wear my black."

"Yes," said Carolus as his car moved forward. "Yes, I think you ought. Thanks very much. Good-bye."

He had driven a quarter of a mile before he remembered that he had been on the way to 'the death house' when Mrs Redlove stopped him. But that could wait. He would not take the chance of another encounter. He would go instead to see 'Mrs Beale at the shop', with whom Florrie Lamplow had been 'very thick' but who 'wouldn't have a lot' to tell him.

She had not, but what little there was he found interesting.

'The shop' was one of two in the village, the other having a wired-off section to serve as a post office and being called by that name. 'The shop' had *Ernest Beale Provisions* in bright letters above its windows, but its stock was meagre. When the shopper ahead of Carolus asked Mrs Beale for some dried fruit she said she was sorry, she had no call for that now, that they all go into Maresfield to the supermarket.

Mrs Beale was a dumpy little woman with a curt business-like manner which rather daunted Carolus who had only the vaguest plans for questioning her. Indeed before he had decided what he should say he found himself addressed.

"Next please," said Mrs Beale, though Carolus was now alone with her in the shop.

"I understand," he said, "that you were a friend of the late Mrs Lamplow?"

"Oh, I'm too upset to talk about that."

"I know. I sympathize. But . . ."

"Yes, dear?" said Mrs Beale peremptorily to a small child who had just entered.

While she was serving, without looking at Carolus, she addressed him again.

"I couldn't say anything. It wouldn't be right. There you are dear, and tell Mum to come and see me about that other. Mind how you go now."

"I just thought . . ." said Carolus.

"No. It would never do for me to say anything. We only heard about it last night."

"She was only found last night. I thought that you, as her friend . . ."

"Yes, but I should never forgive myself. What can I get for you, Sheila?"

She had turned to a tall young woman. But as she weighed some tomatoes for her she continued to speak to Carolus.

"No," she said, "I really couldn't. You must ask some-one else. I wouldn't trust myself."

Carolus tried a direct attack.

"Had she seen much of her friends from Maresfield lately?"

"That's just it," said Mrs Beale. re-arranging some packets of tea.

This was hard going, but Carolus stood his ground while two more customers were served and Mrs Beale seemed to remember his presence.

"Besides, I told Mr Beale this morning, I shan't say any-thing, I said. So it's no good. I don't feel myself about it, and that's a fact. Lying out there. They say she had nothing on but her nightie, poor thing. But it's no good. Yes, boys, what is it?"

Carolus began to lose hope. He decided to wait another five minutes then abandon all possibilities here, at least for the present. But just as he was preparing to leave, Mrs Beale said, across a collection of small groceries she was preparing for a customer—"I'll tell you one thing about her. That'll be eighteen and six altogether, Mrs Rider. Ta. Go in your bag will they? Yes, I'll tell you one thing. She was scared out of her wits to stay in that cottage after Tom had died."

"It is certainly very isolated."

"It wasn't that. She was used to that because she never went out with Tom in the evenings. Good morning, Mr Budd. What can I do for you? All right, I'll put a bit of paper round them. No it wasn't that. It was Something Else. She told me the last time she was in here she didn't mean to stay a minute longer than she could help. That's

143

why when Mrs Redlove said she'd gone off in the night we all thought she had. Fred'll run them round for you if you like, Mr Budd. They're a bit heavy for you. Yes, we never thought any different. But when I heard this morning what had happened, I said to my husband—'There! ' I said, 'what did I tell you? She was scared to be out there all alone, now look what's happened.' "

"She didn't explain at all what frightened her? "

"No. Only that there was Something. I can't say any more. I oughtn't to have said that, really. I'm much too upset by the whole thing. Fancy strangling anyone! You don't know where you are, nowadays, do you? Yes, dear. A shilling's-worth, did Mum say? There you are, then. All I can say is I hope they find who's done it and that he's hanged. Anyone alone like that and their husband only dead a few days. They didn't wait long, I must say."

"When did you last see Mrs Lamplow? " asked Carolus, taking advantage of Mrs Beale's melting reserve.

"Not since the Saturday afternoon when she popped in for a minute on her bicycle. She was worried then. Yes, Mrs Ford? Gone off, had it? I am sorry. It's this hot weather. There's some nice fresh new-laid ones just in; I'm sure you'll find they're all right. Yes, she was worried that afternoon. What's more she had reason to be. Half a pound? Yes. And tea. Let's see, you have the green packets, don't you? Worried out of her life, she was, and I'll tell you why in a moment. No I haven't one left. There's not much call for them, really. What she said was one of Tom's guns was missing."

"She had just noticed it? "

"Yes. She was sure it was there when Tom was taken to hospital, but she couldn't be sure since. Quarter of a pound. Yes. Lovely, isn't it? I suppose the farmers will be wanting rain. Yes. Terrible. I've been so upset I couldn't sleep last night. That's right. One and eight. And it wasn't an ordinary gun either. It was more like a rifle. Tom had worked where there was deer, Florrie said, and the gentleman had given him this. It wasn't until she was just coming out on the Saturday that she noticed it was gone. So you can imagine she was upset. Anyone would be. D'you mind helping yourself then, Miss Pitt? They're just beside you. Yes, two and four, but aren't they beauties? I'll put them in a bag for you. That's why I wasn't surprised when she went off that night, as we thought."

"Tom Lamplow went to hospital a fortnight before that Saturday, didn't he?"

"That's about it. So it was between then and Saturday that she lost that gun. Tom called it a savage."

"You mean it was a Savage 30·30. That is a tricky weapon. You can kill a man at some distance with that. No wonder Mrs Lamplow was worried."

"It wasn't that so much. She scarcely knew the difference. It was the Thought of who might have it. Now what does Mum want? There you are then."

16

" I THOUGHT I saw your car outside," said someone behind Carolus, and he turned to see the craggy features of Mrs Tuck. " I've had to come over and see my niece. They've been On at her."

When they were in the street Mrs Tuck said, " We better go to the Woodmen's because I've got something to tell you. Only we'll go in the Private, which is round the back of the Public, because they'll all be talking about it this morning. It was you found this woman, wasn't it, after me telling you there was Talk about her and Richard? Well, now They're trying to make out he killed her."

Seated in an armchair of the private bar of the Woodmen's Arms, Mrs Tuck swallowed the best part of a milk stout and continued:

"Yes, that's what They're doing. I can tell you because they've been to see my niece and her husband. He's the postman who delivered up at that cottage, so they're asking him this, that and the other. Then one of them who knows me says to my niece, ' It seems funny your aunt should work for him there and your husband should take the letters up to where this woman's murdered '. If that's not trying to put two and two together I don't know what is. Wait till they ask me about it. I shall tell 'em! "

" You don't think the two deaths are connected in any way, then? "

" I don't say that. But I do know Richard didn't kill her. He'd never have thought of such a thing. It wasn't in him. So it's no good Them starting to make out it was. They asked Roger Goode, that's my niece's husband, if he'd ever seen him up there, and Roger told 'em straight he'd never seen anyone up there but these Lamplows themselves. They didn't like that, he said. One of 'em gave him a nasty look, and I shouldn't be surprised if he was to lose his job of postman next. They all work together, you see. I know Them. You fall out with one and it means the lot. It's the same with the bus service. I told a cocky young conductor coming over this morning he wasn't going to tell me where to sit, even if he was dressed up in uniform. ' I'm the conductor on this bus ', he said, so I said ' Are you? ' I said, ' I thought you was a Royal Marine. You can tell Them,' I said, ' that I've had about enough of being told where to sit and where not to sit, and I'll sit where I bloody well like. You tell Them,' I said. ' Language! ' says an old party who ought to've minded his own business. ' You'll get language,' I told him, ' if you start putting your oar in. And it *will* be language,' I said, ' so now then.' I hate 'em. The lot of Them. Anyone would think you was a performing animal, the way They treat you. But about this murder. Can't you find out who done it? I don't like the way They keep on thinking it's Richard."

" I should like to have a talk with Roger Goode."

" I expect he's in the Public now. He'll have finished his round, and a morning like this ten to one he'll have a beer before going for his dinner. I'll ask the landlord."

The postman recognized Carolus.

"You were out there yesterday afternoon," he observed. The perspiration was running off his plump cheeks, but from heat and satisfied thirst, not from perturbation.

"Yes. Tell me, when was the last time you had letters for the Lamplows? Before yesterday, I mean."

"Well, I told you. There was one on the Monday morning. That's how I came to think she'd left. There was no one there and all locked up."

"And before that?"

"It's funny, because she didn't get many letters, but there was a letter for her on Saturday which I took. In the morning it was."

"Did you see Mrs Lamplow?"

"Yes. Stopped and chatted a minute. She was all right."

"Did she say anything about a gun of Tom's which was missing?"

There was a heavy silence in the little room. The fat young man mopped his forehead.

"Now you mention it," he replied at last, "I believe she did say something. Only she called it a rifle."

"Was she perturbed about it?"

This simple question seemed to discomfort Roger Goode.

"She was and she wasn't," he said at last. "I don't think it was the gun so much as who might have taken it. That's what was on her mind."

"You mean, she knew who had taken it?"

"She didn't say so. Not in so many words. But she seemed to be worried about that and having to stay alone in the house."

"Thank you," said Carolus. "What about another pint? Mrs Tuck?"

Goode 'didn't mind' and Mrs Tuck said 'all right'.

"It's a wonder he dares come in here in his uniform," said Mrs Tuck.

"Not supposed to, really."

"There you are! They won't let you breathe next. What's his uniform for, if it's not to wear?"

"That's the rule," said Goode.

"*Rule!* I'd like to give some of Them rules. I wish I'd got hold of that gun of Tom Lamplow's, I'd have a shot at some of 'em."

"Now, Mrs Tuck, you mustn't talk like that," said the landlord, bringing in their drinks.

"Who says I mustn't? I only said what was true. I would like a bang at Them and so would you. Opening time and Closing time, and a copper outside to see you're not two minutes over. I wonder They let you sell beer at all!"

Carolus decided to escape from the private bar as inconspicuously as possible and make for Maresfield, where he now had an urgent mission. He paid for the drinks and took his leave rather hurriedly.

He drove fast now. Something that morning had changed his whole approach, though whether it was a piece of information gained or his own exasperation with the irrepressible loquacity of most witnesses it would be hard to say. Often in previous cases he had been smothered by a haystack of words in his search for the one needle of relevant evidence he sought, but he had never yet had to listen to such a collection as the women here. From the first, Lady Drumbone with her 'cases', to Mrs Beale who was 'too upset' to saying anything but had finally come out with two startling pieces of news, it had been prosies, prosies all the way. The invertebrate Miss Hipps, the luscious Pippa, the enamoured Wilma Day, the embittered Hilda and the chatty Mrs Nodges, the gushing Anita Bourne, Mrs Tuck with her hatred of Them, sensible Olivia Romary and publicity-hungry Daisy Redlove—they had all talked far too readily. But from each he had learned something, and now the pattern was almost complete.

He drove fast, perhaps because he was thinking quickly. He had certain pieces of information to obtain from a number of people he already knew, and his case, he hoped, would be complete. There was nothing vague about the things he wanted to know, a direct question or two in each case should produce the answer. At all costs, he decided, he would avoid long, chatty interviews over cups of tea.

Since it was approaching lunch-time he went first to Hoysden's music shop. This would, presumably, close at one o'clock, and neither Mr Toffin nor Miss Hipps would wish to stay gossiping during their lunch hour.

Mr Toffin, however, could not be approached in the shop but led the way at once to his glass-partitioned office.

"I have another small question for you," said Carolus.

Mr Toffin nodded.

"Anything I can tell you about the business I shall be only too glad. It has been running on oiled wheels. Oiled wheels! "

"This isn't about the business," said Carolus curtly. "On the day before Richard Hoysden's death there was a tennis party at Alan Bourne's house to which you were invited."

Mr Toffin looked puzzled and rather displeased.

"There was, yes," he said. "At Mr Hoysden's particular request both Miss Hipps and I were absent from the business at the same time, not to mention Mr Hoysden himself. 'I hope,' I said to him, 'this is not setting a precedent.' But I felt that as his future part . . . his deput . . . his senior assistant I ought not to refuse."

"What I wanted to know was—did you go upstairs to the room where the men left their blazers, or changed, or whatnot? "

"Certainly not! " said Mr Toffin sharply. "I arrived wearing the correct attire and had no need to change it."

"So you didn't go to the first floor at all? "

"I did not! "

"Thank you, Mr Toffin. Now I should like to see Miss Hipps."

"Her evidence will only confirm mine. But you are at liberty to speak to her."

Miss Hipps insinuated her way into the office, moving

as though she should have been forced as a girl to walk about with books on her head.

"Mr Toffin says you wish to ask me about the tennis party," she said before Carolus could speak. "It was the first time, as a matter of fact, that any of us from the shop had been invited to a private entertainment in the family, and of course it had to be *me*. Mr Toffin said something about our not leaving the shop at the same time, but Mr Hoysden insisted. 'No, I wish Louise to come,' he said . . ."

"I wanted to ask you about something else, Miss Hipps. Do you remember telling me that you had seen Mrs Hoysden going into the Norfolk Hotel with a man?"

"Did I say that? Oh, I shouldn't have, really. It was only once and I . . ."

"When was it?"

"Didn't I tell you? It was that very night!"

"What very night?"

"The night Mr Hoysden . . . the Saturday night . . ."

"A week ago today?"

"Is that all it is? It seems an age."

"You said about nine?"

"Or soon after, yes. I had just come out of the pictures a few doors away."

"You are sure they both entered?"

"Oh, yes. He was carrying their bags."

"*Their* bags?"

"Well, bags. But I don't want to make things worse than they are. He did come out a few minutes later and drive away.

"I was hoping you would say that. Thank you, Miss Hipps."

"I'm only too glad to be of assistance. You see, I *knew* Mr Hoysden . . ."

"Quite. Thanks. Good morning," said Carolus, and with a nod to Toffin as he passed was out of the shop in a moment. In his new and peremptory mood he wanted no more of the coiling sentiments of Miss Hipps.

Outside the door of the shop he ran into Priggley.

" I thought you were swimming? "

" You under-estimate my enthusiasm, sir. I want information for you, and what better source could there be than the redhead? I'm taking her out to lunch."

" Rat," said Carolus, and drove round to the Norfolk.

Hilda was as usual alone. He greeted her cheerfully, but asked at once, " Is Rothsay still in the hotel? "

" I couldn't say, I'm sure," Hilda said inevitably. " I'm not all that interested."

" I particularly want to see him."

" You can, so far as I'm concerned." Then with a rare approach to affability she added, " I suppose I shall have to find out for you."

She returned with Rothsay, who looked anything but affable.

" I hope you're not going to start asking me questions again, old man," he said. " I've told you it's no business of mine."

" I wanted to ask you a small favour," said Carolus blandly.

" Very sorry, old man. Can't manage it. Had a bad couple of days."

" Have you a key of your game-keeper's cottage? "

" Not *my* game-keeper. He worked for a syndicate."

" But you were more on the spot than the others. Have you a key? "

" I believe the agent has. Why? What do you want it for? "

" Just like to borrow it for a few days."

Rothsay seemed to be starting up the engine of his mind, but with the handle. At last he looked at Carolus squarely and said " Have a drink? "

" Thanks," said Carolus, " small whisky and lots of soda."

Rothsay seemed happier now.

" I don't mind asking the agent," he said.

" That's very kind of you."

" I suppose the police will have been in the cottage? "

" Yes. But they'll have finished with it now."

"I'm going back to town this afternoon. I'd better run round to the agent's now. It's only a few yards away."

"Thanks."

So it was with a heavy key in his pocket that Carolus lunched at the Norfolk.

He was soon at work again. What a pity, he thought, that he would have to tackle Slugley at this hour of the day when he would be almost comatose. But there was no help for it.

As he walked across to the block of flats, however, he saw Miss Tripper, Alan's shorthand typist, and as diffidently as possible approached her. Even so, Miss Tripper 'started like a guilty thing Upon a fearful summons', and stood blinking at Carolus, nervous and irresolute.

"You remember me?" smiled Carolus. "We met at Lady Drumbone's. I am enquiring into the circumstances of Richard Hoysden's death."

"Oh, good aft . . ."

"There is one small question I should like to ask you."

"Me? Oh, I hard . . ."

"I wonder if you'd care for a cup of coffee?"

"Coff . . . oh, dear, I'm on my way to the off . . ."

"Just time, surely?"

He piloted her safely into a café, and she sat on the edge of a straight chair.

"It's a question I cannot very well put to Alan Bourne or his wife, though it's a very simple matter and demands no breach of confidence on your part. Do they share a room?"

At first he thought Miss Tripper was going to jump up and walk out, as she obviously longed to do.

"Mr Dee . . . I scarce . . . Very delic . . ." she cried in distress.

"I felt sure that as his confidential secretary you had often been to the house. You could scarcely help knowing."

"Oh, but it's so very pers . . . I cannot bring myself to disc . . ."

Carolus secretly glanced at his watch.

"No need to discuss it," he said as gently as possible.
"Just yes or no."

"But should I be commit . . . Would it be a bre . . ."

"I assure you that it would be no breach of confidence."

"Then ye . . ."

"They did? Invariably?"

Miss Tripper nodded.

"So far as I know invar . . ."

"Thank you. You won't of course mention that I asked
you this?"

"Oh, I couldn't poss . . . On such a sub . . . My employ . . . Improp . . ."

"That's right, then."

She was delighted to rise and lead the way to the street.

"Good-bye, Miss Tripper," said Carolus.

"Good . . ." said Miss Tripper and fled.

Slugley, as Carolus feared, looked at him with slothful
eyes. But the memory of Carolus's trip, though it did not
animate him, at least brought a distant "Arf noon" from
between his fingers as he absently levered at a lower molar.

"When I saw you the other day," Carolus began at once,
"I was going to ask you about Richard Hoysden's car in
the park. But your telling me about the Mercedes put it
right out of my mind. Did you notice it that evening?"

"Yers, but I can't say what time or anything about it,
because it being one of the regular ones out there I
shouldn't, should I? I'd only have noticed a car if it was
out of the way, like the Mercedes."

Something in Slugley's flaccid face warned Carolus not
to abandon the conversation too quickly. Though Slugley's
dull eye was on the traffic, Carolus felt almost sure that
there was more to come.

"Tell you what, though," said Slugley at last. "Talking
about cars, I was woke up that night. Yers, getting on for
two o'clock it must have been. Car started up and drove
away from right outside the window of the little room at
the back of where I sleep. Just where Mr Hoysden kept
his Hillman."

"Was it his Hillman?"

"Might have been. I couldn't tell. You don't think I was going to get up and look, do you?"

"Did you hear it return?"

"Yers. Woke me up again. But I can't say what time that was. Not long before it began to get light I should think."

There was another flicker and conjuring trick, and Slugley returned to his distended boa-constrictor's contemplation of the traffic.

Only one more, thought Carolus, not without satisfaction. It was not long before he was sitting in the drawing-room of Mount Edgcumbe awaiting the entrance of Anita Bourne.

When she had made it he spoke very politely.

"I really hoped to find your husband at home, Mrs Bourne. There's a small detail I want to clear up, but you can tell me as easily as he, and that will save him being troubled at his office."

Mrs Bourne bowed graciously.

"It's this. Did anything happen to disturb him that Saturday night? A phone call or anything?"

"Nothing! He slept as usual as peacefully as a child."

"You would have known if he was called down or anything?"

"Oh, yes. I am far the lighter sleeper. He rose rather early, as you know, because he was going to see poor Richard."

"What time did you both retire?" ventured Carolus, thinking that 'retire' was just the word for Anita Bourne.

"It was well after midnight, I fear. We had entertained some friends for dinner."

"Thank you, Mrs Bourne."

"Let me ring for . . ."

"No thanks. Really. I must run."

Either, thought Carolus, she had spoken the truth or she was one of the most accomplished and barefaced liars he had ever met.

154

FROM breakfast next morning Carolus was summoned to the telephone.

"It's Lady Drumbone," said Mrs Stick with the stoical air of one who has now abandoned herself to the inevitable.

The lady politician's rich voice made a loud contralto assault on Carolus's eardrum.

"Mr Deene, are you responsible for this?"

"Responsible for what?" asked Carolus irritably. He was never at his most affable in the early morning.

"Haven't you read the newspapers?"

"Certainly not. I haven't finished the crossword yet. Let's keep our sense of proportion."

"This is no joke, Mr Deene. If I find that you are in any way involved I shall . . . I shall report it to your head-master."

"Yes, do that, whatever it is. His address is Pension Le Balmoral, Ostend. He'd be delighted to hear from you. And now would you control your hysteria sufficiently to tell me what is *in* the newspapers?"

"I shall leave you to discover that for yourself if you don't already know. When you have done so would you please come over and see me immediately?"

"I shall be over this morning. I'll certainly look in."

Carolus called Mrs Stick.

"Would you ask Stick to go round to the newsagent's shop and get me all the popular papers? The Daily Horror, The Daily Wail, The Daily Explosion and The Daily Smirch."

"I hope there's nothing about you in them, sir," said Mrs Stick severely. "I managed to talk my sister round last time, but if she was to read again that we work where you're mixed up in murders and that, I don't know what she wouldn't say. She's married to a gentleman in the

Undertaking and always has been most respectable. Living in Battersea as she is, it would never do for people to know anything about her sister."

" If Stick gets the papers we shall see, shan't we? "

When Stick returned and Carolus had had time to look at the headlines, he saw what Lady Drumbone had meant. The existence of the tape-recording had become known, and short of accusing Lady Drumbone of murder, the crime reporters had said about everything which might damage her. Steering between libel and contempt of court they had succeeded in portraying a woman feverishly covering up evidence which involved her family and trying to save her name by subterfuge or, as they hinted, bribery. " No Prosecution Contemplated " said one headline, referring to a charge of suppression of evidence. This suggested that Lady Drumbone was even now paying out large sums to preserve herself from a term in Holloway. The matter of Florrie Lamplow's death was dealt with in a separate but adjacent column, and no reader could escape the conclusion that the family had been aware of Richard Hoysden's homicidal tendencies, and finding that they had had this appalling outcome, had combined to conceal the whole thing.

Furthermore, it was said that the inquest on the game-keeper's wife was being held on the following day, and suggested that Hoysden's confession should form part of the evidence at this. Lady Drumbone, it was hoped, would be cross-examined and it would be known why her nephew's confession had been hitherto suppressed.

All this was presented with the usual distorted photographs of Lady Drumbone herself, Richard, Pippa, Alan and Keith. There were interviews with Mr Toffin (" Mr Hoysden was always a perfect gentleman though somewhat unbusinesslike "), Miss Hipps (" It was to me he always turned in trouble "), and Mrs Redlove (" I was her closest friend "). The game-keeper's cottage appeared and a picture of the clearing in which Florrie's body was found (" Favourite resort of the Drumbone family, it was here that Mrs Lamplow's mangled body was discovered six days after her murder "). Column after column of red-hot newsprint under flaming headlines told the story of " Hushed-Up Horrors at Maresfield ".

It was not difficult to guess how news of the existence of the tape-recording had leaked out, in fact 'leaked' was an inadequate word—an undammed rush would have been more expressive. As he had pointed out as early as last Sunday evening, eight people were then aware of it, and it had since been handed to the police. A local reporter and correspondent of London papers would be a poor performer indeed, if he did not hear of it, and skilled questioners would have done the rest. Doubtless the fact that Carolus's own name nowhere appeared had convinced Lady Drumbone that he was responsible.

The attack, indirect as it was, plainly had Lady Drumbone for its objective. 'Hoist with her own petard', thought Carolus grimly as he drove over. But he smiled to himself as he wondered what kind of a reception he would get.

When Lady Drumbone entered the lounge Wilma Day was, as the Court Circular says, 'in attendance'.

'In spite of your impertinence to me on the telephone this morning," began Lady Drumbone, " I have decided to give you a chance to explain yourself."

"Oh, haven't you wired the headmaster?" asked Carolus in disappointment.

"I have postponed that till I have seen you."

"You should have. He would love an excuse to fly over for the last act."

" Mr Deene, did you or did you not, inform the press of the existence of that tape-recording? "

As Carolus was about to reply the telephone rang and Wilma hurried to it.

"It's one of those ex-prisoners from Dartmoor who say they were used as human guinea pigs for a serum and are now suffering from poliomyelitis, tuberculosis and hay fever."

"That," said Lady Drumbone, " will have to wait. Now, Mr Deene? "

"I haven't seen anyone from the press," said Carolus. "I agree that the whole hu-ha is rather silly."

"Silly! It is the outcome of cold-blooded malice and jealousy. I accept your word that the information did not come from you, and I have my suspicions about its source."

"It had to come out, you know. The press isn't asleep. A story like that was bound to break."

"Nevertheless, someone here in Maresfield must be responsible for its first revelation. I think I know who that is."

"Oh. Who?"

The telephone sounded again.

"It's the *Sunday Clarion*," said Wilma. "Have you finished your article on The Martyrdom of Mau-Mau?"

"Tell them I have other, more personal matters to attend to."

"They say they know that. But they need the article tomorrow."

"Tell them I'll see what I can do."

"You were telling me whom you suspect of sneaking," said Carolus.

"A man called Slugley. The porter in the block of flats over Richard's shop. It has lately come to my knowledge that he is the brother of a Sergeant Slugley whose inhuman brutality to a squad of recruits I exposed. The men were tortured and forced to undergo various hideous privations. Sergeant Slugley was reduced to the ranks and his brother has declared a vendetta against me."

"I should not have thought he had the energy."

"No great energy is required for a treacherous action of this kind. The problem is—what can be done to check it?"

"The newspaper campaign? Nothing, I imagine."

"It was to avoid a situation of this kind that I engaged your services, Mr Deene."

"It was to discover the truth that I took on the case."

"Have you discovered the truth?"

"I think so. I have to obtain confirmation, which I am preparing to do."

"And what, may I ask, *is* the truth?"

"Richard didn't murder Florrie Lamplow, if that is any help to you."

Lady Drumbone's air of extreme surprise gave her away. "He *didn't*?"

"Certainly not."

She paused a moment to realize the full implications of this. Carolus was tempted to wink to Wilma Day, who was behind her.

"You can prove this?"

"Only by naming her murderer, which I am not yet prepared to do."

"But you are certain?"

"In my own mind, yes."

A decision was being made and Lady Drumbone rose to her feet to announce it.

"Miss Day," she said, "kindly go to the other telephone and call the offices of all the newspapers who have printed this libellous stuff. Tell them that I will see their representatives here at five o'clock today. Tell them that all members of my family will be present. Tell them that Mr Carolus Deene, a private investigator of some repute, has startling new light to throw on the matter. Then please see that Mr and Mrs Alan Bourne, Mrs Hoysden, my nephew Keith and my niece Mrs Romary are present."

Wilma left them together and Carolus smiled.

"You may scotch the snake," he said, "but don't imagine for a moment that you'll kill it."

"At least it should teach these persons not to take Richard's guilt for granted as they have done. You are prepared to tell them in uncompromising terms what you have told me?"

"Yes, though it will bring Gorringer post haste from Ostend, probably lose me my housekeeper and certainly irritate the police."

"I have always found, Mr Deene, that the truth is its own reward."

"Have you now? I shall come here shortly before five

and make the statement you require. But I shall say no more, however I'm questioned."

Lady Drumbone bowed.

"Mr Deene," she said, "there is another matter on which I must speak to you. I gather you have seen a certain amount of my nephew Keith?"

"He has been very helpful."

"I trust you have done nothing to encourage his absurd attempts to flirt with my secretary, Wilma Day?"

"No business of mine," said Carolus, "but I think they are sincerely in love."

"They are both far too young to consider it. I have told Keith flatly that I will countenance neither that nor his equally unreasonable wish to start a repertory theatre here."

"Pity," said Carolus. "He seems interested. But that is a family matter. I will come here before five, Lady Drumbone."

Carolus kept his word. At ten to five he braved the stomach-searing swiftness of the lift and found the family assembled. They treated him with unusual cordiality, perhaps because he was to help clear Richard's name.

"I do not know whether this is a time of day when you wish to drink, Mr Deene. If so please help yourself."

A collection of bottles had been set ready for the press conference.

"We hear you know who killed Florrie," said Alan, "but that you want confirmation."

"Yes. I'm going to stay in her cottage for a few days."

Olivia Romary smiled.

"You think the murderer will return to the scene of his crime?" she suggested.

"Something like that, perhaps," said Carolus.

"I say, I wish you'd let me come with you," pleaded Keith. "Remember I know the place well."

"No. I've got to be alone there, I'm afraid."

"I shouldn't care for it," remarked Pippa. "Only a few yards from where a murder was committed."

160

"Or at least where a corpse was found," said Olivia, who read crime novels.

There were only half-a-dozen press representatives when all had gathered, and Alan, who seemed to be conducting the affair, wisely kept it informal. Family and press sat about the room unsegregated, and though only four of the six joined Carolus in having a drink, it seemed at first that good humour would be maintained all round. But gradually the room fell silent as Alan began to explain.

"We think it's rather unfair of you to suggest that evidence was deliberately suppressed. I want to explain that it was I who found the recording and I take full responsibility for not having handed it in at once. But you must remember that no murder had then been discovered, and I frankly believed the thing was a piece of raving."

He was stopped there by someone who asked if he had a copy of the words used by Richard.

"No," he said blandly, "I haven't."

Almost certainly, thought Carolus, this was true. Miss Tripper had not waited to find and insert a carbon and Alan certainly had not got the typescript which was in his, Carolus's, pocket.

"At what point did you in fact hand it over, Mr Bourne?" Alan was asked.

"As soon as I realized its importance."

"But not in time for the inquest?"

"There was a good deal of confusion," explained Alan. "It had been a great shock to all of us."

"Lady Drumbone, may I ask if you knew of this recording?"

"I am prepared to answer questions," said Lady Drumbone rising to this, "not to face an inquisition."

"Did you know of it, Mrs Hoysden?"

"Yes," said Pippa, "I didn't take it seriously. It was quite absurd. Richard was incapable of killing anyone."

The first camera flash showed Pippa looking very handsome as she answered.

The conference continued for about fifteen minutes. A

mistake, thought Carolus, who saw the news angles multiplying with every word. But he said nothing until Alan drew him in.

"There is one rather important aspect of this," said Alan. "Mr Carolus Deene has been investigating the affair and has something interesting to say."

Carolus felt himself under the bored scrutiny of Fleet Street.

"Not much," he said. "It's something that ought to have been obvious from the first. Richard Hoysden didn't kill Florrie Lamplow. That's all."

"You mean to say he had nothing to do with her death?"

"I said he did not kill her. Let us respect our words."

"It was just a coincidence then? She was strangled on the night on which he committed suicide saying that he had just strangled a woman. Pure coincidence?"

"No comment," said Carolus maddeningly.

"Do you know who did?"

"I think so."

"Have you informed the police?"

"No."

"Are you suppressing evidence, Mr Deene?"

"No. The police are in possession of all the facts as I know them."

"What makes you think he did not kill her?"

"I don't think. I know it. But I couldn't convince you and don't intend to try."

"This is a very extraordinary attitude. Are you going to name the murderer?"

"In due course, yes, unless the police have arrested him or her first."

"Or *her*? Do you think a woman could have strangled Mrs Lamplow?"

"No comment."

"Who are you acting for in this case?"

"No one. I'm interested."

"You're saying that it doesn't matter that the coroner

never heard that recording because what Richard Hoysden said in it wasn't true?"

"I'm not saying anything about the coroner."

"Do you think, then, that the recording was a fake? That it wasn't made by Hoysden?"

"I have no means of knowing. I never knew Richard Hoysden."

"Do you think the police are making a mistake?"

"I know nothing about the police."

There followed a number of personal questions. Carolus was asked his age, profession, criminological experience, and so on. Flash bulbs flared again. Then, with extraordinary precipitation, the press left.

"It seems to me, Mr Deene," said Lady Drumbone, "that you were seeking publicity for yourself."

"At all events," said Carolus, "I shall certainly have it. I expect the headmaster within forty-eight hours."

18

"REALLY, sir," said Priggley at breakfast on Monday morning, "you shouldn't do these things suddenly. Where on earth did you get it?"

'It' referred, as even Carolus could not pretend to ignore, to a check suit he was wearing, so vivid and blatant that it made Rothsay's clothes discreet by comparison. Even Mrs Stick seemed to start and almost drop the tray she was carrying.

"Anything wrong, Mrs Stick?"

"It's not for me to say, sir," returned the little woman primly. "Only I must own I'd like to know where it came from. It wasn't in your wardrobe yesterday."

"Oh, this?" said Carolus trying to carry it off.

"I shall have to warn Stick. If he was to see it unexpected it might bring on one of his old attacks. I don't know whatever made you get it."

"I shan't be in, tonight, Mrs Stick. I shall want a bag with one of my other suits in."

"I should think you would," said Mrs Stick. "You couldn't wear that all the time, could you?"

Something was happening to her mouth, and Priggley maintained afterwards that it was a smile.

"Tell me," said Carolus, when Mrs Stick had left them, "as a nice healthy boy with a pen-knife, a piece of string and a few horse-chestnuts in your pocket, could you fix up a microphone and amplifier?"

"Fix up?"

"Yes. I want a microphone in one place and the loud-speaker concealed some distance away. Is that beyond your capacities?"

"Of course not. But what on earth are you going to try now? No sensational stuff, sir, please. You know it doesn't suit you. Working things out in an armchair is your line. Every time you've tried to do anything violent it has ended in disaster."

"What's violent about a microphone? Can you or can't you fix it up?"

"I can. But I don't like the sound of it. I don't trust you in this neck-or-nothing mood."

"It's a very mild neck-or-nothing," said Carolus when they were out of the house. "We'll buy the things we want here in Newminster. Can you tell me exactly what's necessary?"

"Yes. You've got a spare car battery, haven't you? What distance will the mike be from the amplifier?"

"Say twenty yards."

"And where will the amplifier be?"

"Say in a tree."

"I begin to understand. The game-keeper's cottage?"

Carolus nodded.

"That'll be easy."

Their purchases made, they went to a large outfitters' shop, where Carolus was greeted with something like rapture by the manager.

"A perfect fit if I may say so, sir. And the pattern is

the last word in chic. Perhaps your friend would like something similar? "

" God forbid," said Priggley. " I've had misery enough walking down the High Street beside this one. Every dog in the place started barking."

" Ah, fond of your little joke, I see," said the manager unsmiling, turning to Carolus. " What can we do for you today, sir? "

" I want the dummy in the window. The seated one."

The manager laughed, loudly but not heartily.

" Ah, there you are! " he said. " I could see when you came in last night you liked your joke. The dummy in the window! Very funny indeed, sir."

" I don't mind whether I borrow, hire or buy the thing. But I want that particular one."

" Oh dear, oh dear! You mustn't make me laugh so, sir."

" I'm serious," said Carolus.

The manager suddenly sobered.

" You mean? "

" I mean I need that dummy for a day or two."

" If you are serious, sir, I fear I must refuse. It would be as much as my job's worth. Each branch is only allowed the four dummies. What happens if one of the directors comes down and sees it missing? I shouldn't know what to say."

" Say it fell in love with one of the female dummies in the dress-shop next door," suggested Priggley, " and that they're living together in sin."

The manager remained solemn.

" It would never do," he murmured.

" Only three days," said Carolus.

" No, no, sir . . ."

" It would be worth a fiver to me," said Carolus, in a low voice. " After all, you could say it was being repaired."

" It would cost more like a tenner to repair," said the manager quickly.

" A tenner, then."

" When would you want it? "

" Now," said Carolus.

" That means changing it."

" Well? "

" I should have to ask Mr Winkley to do that. I don't think it's very nice to expect the young lady who does the window to do it."

" Why not? "

" It has to be Undressed, you see," said the manager.

" But surely it isn't . . . it hasn't got . . ."

" Oh, no, sir. Certainly not. But I feel it's *nicer* for a man to do it, Mr Winkley! "

It was half an hour before Carolus and Priggley carried a very odd-looking package from the shop. Armed with this and the purchases already made they drove out of Newminster.

" But I want to get to Flogmore without going through Maresfield," said Carolus. " It means a detour of more than twenty miles, but it can't be helped."

When they entered the cottage they found it in some confusion.

" Looks as though the Law have done their job," said Priggley. " I'd like to have seen them at work—finger-prints and all."

" Don't gibe at finger-prints," said Carolus, " we're going to depend on them ourselves."

" Sunk to that, have you? You'll be buying a microscope next. Where do you want the amplifier? "

" Fairly high up in one of those trees in front of the house."

" You seem pretty sure the fly will walk into the parlour."

" Yes, I'm pretty sure."

" But how do you know what route it will take? It might come from behind the house."

" I don't think so. Only a few people know that route. Besides, the windows all look out to the front."

" Yes. There's that. What about the big chestnut tree? "

" It'll do. Now I'm going to leave you here to do the job. I want the mike in that upstairs room on the right. And don't be seen if you can help it. You'd hear a car from some distance so watch out for anyone on foot. If you are disturbed try to lock the cottage and get out of the way."

"Good. How long will you be?"

"Some time. I'm so pleased with this suit that I want it to be seen by almost everyone in Maresfield."

"Once seen, never forgotten."

"That's what I thought."

"It's the most disgusting exhibitionism, but I suppose you've got some reason for it."

"I have."

As he hoped, Mrs Redlove was in wait for him at the end of the cart-track.

"I didn't much care for that picture you put in," she said, "and there wasn't only a little about what I said."

"I thought it was good," said Carolus.

"I've thought of a bit more I never told you. You write this down. 'Mrs Redlove says dead woman lived in terror.'"

"But did she?"

"From what I can hear she didn't like being in that house alone after her husband died."

"Has anyone been up there lately?"

"Not since Friday they haven't. It was Friday they came to see me. You should have seen the pictures they took! I don't know why they haven't come out in the papers. There was one of Arthur and Margaret that must have been sweetly pretty, and one ever so good of my husband, I'm sure, because he had his blue serge on. But there you are. It's all about that Lady Drumbone. I suppose it's being a 'Lady'. I've never set eyes on her, anyway, so I don't believe she had much to do with it. You could put that in. 'Mrs Redlove of Brook Cottage, Flogmore, says Lady Drumbone a stranger'."

"You're sure no car has been up to the game-keeper's cottage since Friday?"

"Of course I'm sure. After what's happened I'm not missing anything, I can tell you. I saw you go in half an hour ago and that's all there has been."

"I shall be back later."

"Then I'll see if I can remember anything. There's that

prize Margaret won last year. She could be holding it in her hand. Mrs Redlove's prize-winning daughter remembers killer's victim.'"

"Charming," said Carolus and escaped.

It was fairly late in the afternoon when Carolus returned, having finished his piece of 'disgusting exhibitionism'. When he reached the cottage he carefully turned the car so that its nose pointed towards the track. He had brought a supply of food and drink, and Priggley set on this ravenously, not having eaten since breakfast.

"I've cleared the place up a bit," he told Carolus between mouthfuls. "I don't suppose you will want to sleep and don't find the bed very inviting, but I've put a couple of comfortable chairs in the room where the mike is. That's fixed, too, and I've tested it for sound."

"Good. No one been around?"

"No one at all."

"I'm going to change," said Carolus.

"I should imagine you'd be relieved. Though do you know I'm getting rather to like that chessboard you're wearing?"

"I'm glad. I wanted it to be glaring but not funny."

"Fair enough."

"There's nothing very funny about this thing, really. Even the purpose this suit is to serve is not hilarious."

"In fact, I had gathered that. It's your intention to trap a murderer, no less?"

"And a particularly nasty one."

"I shall watch it with interest."

"If you are going to stay here tonight it will be on one condition. You will give me your word that in no circumstances, in no circumstances at all, you understand, will you leave the small bedroom. It looks from the front of the house, so if there is anything to see you will see it. But I must have your word of honour that you will not leave that room."

"Drama?" asked Priggley.

"Possibly."

"It's about time. All right, I promise. Are you sure there will be fun and games tonight?"

"No. It may be tomorrow. Or just possibly the next night. But I think tonight."

"How can you be so sure that he . . ."

"Or she."

"I don't take that seriously in a strangling case. Anyway I shall say 'he'. How can you be so sure he'll walk into a carefully prepared trap?"

"I know this murderer."

"Why not get out that mantrap from the shed and set it?"

"No need. This is just as sure. It was that unpleasant-looking piece of mechanism which gave me the idea, however."

"Don't say you're going to make an arrest?"

"Oh, no. I should have no authority to do that."

"Anyway, since you're determined to be so damned mysterious let me get what I can straight. In the language of the kind of books I fear you must have been reading, we 'keep vigil' tonight?"

"We do."

"And the murderer will approach?"

"Yes. Almost certainly."

"On which we grab him?"

"No. *You* remain in that room."

"You grab him then?"

"No."

"What's the idea of it all, in that case?"

"Identification," said Carolus.

"I suppose I shall have to be satisfied with that. What about our dummy?"

"When I've changed you can dress it. Unless you think that wouldn't be very nice."

"In the chessboard?"

"Exactly."

"Where does he sit?"

"In the room downstairs."

" With a light? "

" Of course."

" I begin to see. I rather like it."

" Thank you, Priggley. I was afraid you would find it, in your favourite word, corny."

" It is, of course, but it has that childish ingenuity about it which will probably work."

When the dummy was dressed in the loud suit Carolus had been wearing all day and placed with its back almost but not quite square to the open window, a book open before it and a paraffin lamp lit—though it was scarcely dusk —it presented from outside a curiously realistic spectacle.

" Hair a bit too blond for you," said Priggley. " We must get a shadow across it. Otherwise it really is indistinguishable from here."

" Let's walk up the track to the point from which one first sees the cottage."

They did so. From there the illusion was complete.

" That's it then," said Carolus. " We take up our positions."

They went to the upstairs room of the cottage.

" Make yourself comfortable. We may have hours to wait. No light—not even a cigarette. We shall probably hear a car engine first, but that's by no means certain."

" The weakness of the whole thing seems to be this," said Priggley, " that he will scarcely believe you could be so idiotic as to sit there making a target for him."

" People believe their own eyes. A few minutes later they may realize that they have been fooled, but the first instant reaction is what counts."

" Yes. I see that. But we shan't be able to see him. It's a dark night."

" We don't need to see."

" I give it up."

" That's best. From now on talk quietly. Back and front doors bolted? "

" Yes."

" All windows shut? "

"Yes."

Their 'vigil' began. After what seemed a considerable time, Priggley said:

"He does know you're here?"

"Oh, yes."

"And he knows you know who he is?"

"Yes. I think so."

"Then how can you possibly be so sure he'll come? What motive can he have?"

"Desperation."

"You mean—to *plead*?"

"Oh, no."

"To kill, then?"

"Of course."

"It's fantastic. There are a thousand things against it."

"What, for instance?"

"How does he know that you're the only person to know his identity?"

"But I am."

"Then he has got to be absent during the time it takes him to come here. He could surely be traced through that?"

"This murderer is an expert at alibis. Besides—all right, we'll call him 'he', if you like—the fact that he comes here tonight need not implicate him at all. He might be coming out of anxiety for me. Even when he has killed me he has only got to say he found me dead. Report it at once. Heard I was coming here, came out to help and found me dead. That might be accepted from any respectable person."

"Is he respectable?"

"Very."

"I see what you mean. It does begin to look more promising. But suppose you had told someone, me for instance, who it was. Even though he succeeded in killing you it wouldn't have served much purpose."

"Every purpose. Because I haven't a scrap of concrete proof. The only proof will be given tonight. All my evidence is circumstantial. If he killed me and got away with my murder he would never be charged at all. He knows that. His choice is a simple one. To kill me and be safe on the one hand or to let me live and hang on the other."

"But surely, sir," whispered Priggley excitedly, "he must know you wouldn't stay here without taking precautions? That's the crux of the whole thing. He *knows* you're expecting him, he *knows* you know he means to kill you. He can't think you're so stupid as to be here without protection?"

"No," said Carolus. "But he is pretty sure he can defeat my precautions. *You see, he has the means to do so.* Think that one out."

The most nerve-racking thing about that wait was the darkness. There was silence, too, except for an owl, for it was a still and heavy night. But the darkness was hostile. From their window they could just see the vague shape of the chestnut tree in which was the amplifier, but nothing of the track. It would be possible for anyone to reach the windows beneath them without being seen.

"Have you got a gun?" asked Rupert presently.

"Yes, but if I have to use it the whole thing will have failed. The only charge would be one against me. What's the time?"

"Eleven-thirty. I'm enjoying this. This is good. Why can't you do this more often?"

When interruption came it was ear-splitting. There were several phases all within a single second. There was an explosion and a shattering of glass below them, then a thud within the house.

Very coolly Carolus spoke into the microphone.

"Drop that gun, you fool! You are being covered from three points." The words blared out in the night with an eerie sound like someone shouting into a cave.

Carolus motioned Priggley to stay where he was and opening the window peered out.

"Now listen," he commanded.

172

It seemed a long time before they heard anything. When it came it was faint but clearly distinguishable. A car on the road was started up and driven away at speed.

"You've let him go!" said Priggley.

But there was no time to answer. Smoke was rising from the staircase.

"God! The lamp! Out of here," shouted Carolus. "No, not down the stairs. Where's that window?"

Priggley opened the window by which he had entered the cottage three days earlier and they clambered out. The cottage was fairly alight.

"With that thatch it won't last half an hour. Come on, we've got to find that gun."

"Oughtn't we . . ."

"Hell, nothing matters but that."

"The car far enough away?" asked Priggley.

"Yes. Find the gun. Before anyone comes. Find it. It's the only thing of any importance."

But it was not hard to find. It lay in the centre of the path, at the very point they had discovered that afternoon from which the cottage came into sight.

"Must have dropped it like a hot brick. That loud-speaker would have shaken anyone, overhead, suddenly like that."

Using his handkerchief Carolus gingerly lifted the gun, a Savage 30-30, and returned to his car.

The cottage blazed furiously.

"I like a fire as much as anyone, but there's no time for that."

"Where to?" asked Priggley.

"The home of the CID man in charge."

"It's one-thirty."

"Couldn't care less. He's got to take the finger-prints on this. What do you think it was all for—dummy, loud-speaker, the lot? Surely you realized? A set of finger-prints which will hang a murderer. A little concrete proof at last. I told you I wanted identification. And you talked about letting him get away."

19

Mrs Stick was evidently beyond speech next morning, and silently handed Carolus the headmaster's telegram.

"I thought so," said Carolus to Priggley as he read it. "But he certainly doesn't waste words. *Outraged Meet Norfolk Hotel Maresfield 10 a.m. tomorrow Gorringer.* It's past ten now so we shall find him tearing his hair."

Carolus, however, finished his coffee and smilingly told Mrs Stick that he would not be in to lunch. Her lips remained firmly shut.

Rupert Priggley knew better than to ask questions at this point. He had watched while Carolus continued for ten minutes to ring at the door of Detective Inspector Bowler's house at two o'clock that morning, and had heard the brief summary Carolus gave him as he handed over the gun.

"I shall require a full statement from you," said Bowler severely, and Carolus had promised it, also choosing the Norfolk as a meeting place this morning.

If Mr Gorringer had been tearing his hair he showed no sign of it as he stood squarely on the hearthrug of the Residents' Lounge awaiting Carolus. His mood seemed to be one of Olympian and icy calm tempered with haughty disillusionment.

"Good morning, Deene," he said in a sad and lofty voice. "I have, as you see, been forced to abandon my hard-earned repose to come here and cope with this disaster. I felt it my duty to see what fragments of the school's reputation might yet be salvaged."

"What disaster? *Not* Hollingbourne?"

"It is useless, on this occasion, for you to be evasive, Deene. I, nay, the world has seen the newspapers of yesterday in which your name is blazoned—yes, sir, blazoned—

as that of an investigator whose views run counter to those held by the police."

"I thought you would be delighted when I tried to clear Lady Drumbone's nephew."

"But at what cost! 'Senior History Master at the Queen's School, Newminster', I quote but one of the descriptions. What do you suppose the Governing Body will say to this?"

"You've heard nothing yet, headmaster. Wait till I make my full statement to the police, presently. It really *is* a bit of a shocker, this case. Another murder was attempted last night."

"And who," asked Mr Gorringer in his Jehovah voice, "who was the intended victim?"

"I was," said Carolus. "But you'll hear all that presently. When Detective Inspector Bowler arrives."

Mr Gorringer sank into a chair.

"There are moments, Deene, when I feel that the responsibilities of my position are too great."

"Have a drink," suggested Carolus. "I could do with one myself. I was up till almost daybreak. Priggley, see if you can find a waiter."

A little restored, Mr Gorringer asked at what time Bowler would arrive.

"Soon, I hope. But I had to pull him out of bed in the small hours too, poor chap."

"Meanwhile, I should like to be er . . . put in the picture."

"Good. Priggley will go right through the case with you while I just check my notes."

They were interrupted some time later by the rather violent entry of Mrs Tuck.

"I been looking everywhere for you. D'you know what They've done now? Gone and arrested . . ."

"Now, Mrs Tuck, I want you as a favour to keep your temper and say nothing more. This is Mr Gorringer, the headmaster of the Queen's School, Newminster."

The headmaster's bow might be described as steely.

175

"What'll They do next, I'd like to know? It's the same with one I met in the hall just now all dressed up like a Turkish admiral who tried to stop me coming in. Pretty soon told *him*. I suppose they'll arrest me next."

She clearly had no intention of leaving, but sat down firmly, and in answer to Carolus's invitation accepted a stout.

Seeing some facial contortions of the headmaster's which he took to be interrogative, Carolus said briefly that Mrs Tuck was a friend of his. This did little to allay Mr Gorringer's anxiety.

Bowler arrived looking businesslike, was briefly introduced to Mr Gorringer, and said, "Now I should like this statement of yours, Mr Deene."

"It seems that Deene has a great deal to account for," said Mr Gorringer. Then turning to Bowler he explained: "As his employer I feel to some extent implicated, Inspector. I make no secret of the fact that it was I who first suggested that he might be of some assistance to Lady Drumbone, but I little thought that it would lead to such a situation as this! Another corpse! And now, I hear, a further attempt at bloodshed! I begin to ask where this kind of thing will end. Are we, even here, by the fireside as it were, of an English inn, to consider ourselves secure?"

At that moment there was the sound of violent scuffling outside the door and Mr Gorringer jumped to his feet. But when the door was flung open it revealed Mrs Redlove, somewhat dishevelled, and attended by a young reporter from the local paper.

Her finger shot out at Carolus.

"That's him!" she shouted, like the monks of Rheims. "That's the murderer! I should know him anywhere! Saying he was a newspaper man and having me put on my bluey-emerald! He was up there yesterday again, because I saw him and his car went off after the shot was fired last night. You write that down," she said to the reporter, who complied. "'Mrs Redlove of Brook Cottage, Flogmore, Unmasks Murderer'. It was him set the house on fire, too, to destroy the evidence so there's nothing left of it now only ashes. You can say that. 'Mrs Redlove finds only ashes where neighbour's house once stood '."

Mr Gorringer, conscious of his importance, rose to deal with this interruption.

"I fear you're making a mistake, madam," he pronounced. But he got no further.

"It's no mistake," said Mrs Redlove, "because I seen him with my own eyes. Photographer, he told me, and Margaret crying her eyes out because he never came and Arthur spilling jam on his new suit. He was up there yesterday doing I don't know what, and I see his car go off after the other one. Have you got your camera ready? Because someone must go for the police. 'Mrs Redlove denounces murderer. Arrest of Flogmore Woods killer '."

Slowly and unwillingly Bowler rose to explain patiently that he was in charge of the case and that if Mrs Redlove had some information for him she could call at his office later. It took some minutes to quieten her, but eventually she left, disappointed rather than reassured.

"Now, Mr Deene," said Bowler.

Carolus lit a cheroot.

"You won't need any very long-winded explanations here. But before I just run over the few points I have noticed I should like to see how the facts look to someone who knows them all and is accustomed to this sort of case. Priggley, will you take a pencil and paper and jot down your considered answers to these questions. *Richard Hoysden's death.* (a) Accident? (b) Suicide? (c) Murder? *Mrs Lamplow's death.* Same three choices. And in both cases, if accident, how? If suicide, why? If murder, by whom?[1] All right, keep that till later."

"To the point, Deene!" cried Mr Gorringer.

"The point, of course, was the tape-recording. The

[1] The reader may derive amusement from doing the same, but only *if he doesn't cheat!* A critic recently accused me of being "frantically serious" about the problem set in one of these books. I can't quite see the point of a who-dun-it unless the thing is laid out as fair and square as a crossword.—L.B.

whole case turns on that. As soon as I heard it I was interested, for I perceived at once that I was dealing with no ordinary intelligence. I also realized that Richard Hoysden had been murdered."

Mr Gorringer could be relied on for an interpolation.

"Murdered, was he? " he gasped.

"Of course. For the first thing that was noticeable about the words of that recording was that *they were read*. Richard Hoysden was not a literary type, but even if he were it would obviously be impossible for him to deliver such an oration as that, with apt and word-perfect quotations from Othello, unless he had a script. A man about to shoot himself is unlikely to bother about fine phraseology, but if he has an exhibitionistic desire to display it, he must write down what he wants to say. According to Alan Bourne, who found the body, no script was there.

"The next noticeable point about that confession was the way it started. " Oh, I killed her all right . . ." What does that suggest to you? That it was an answer to other words, that is to say that what Richard was reading was *a speech from a play*. Its whole tenor suggests that, apart from anything else, and although I had not the advantage of having known Richard, I gathered that this was what the voice used in the recording suggested, too. I remember Pippa's very expressive remark 'the voice was Richard's all right, but it was not Richard speaking'. I also remembered Toffin saying that Richard had 'an unusually rich and dramatic voice'.

"Then there was that very important expletive at the end. 'Hell! ' said Richard when he had finished reading, not in the tone he had been using, but in his own natural manner. Again, to quote his wife, when I asked if it wasn't out of keeping—'To me it's the only thing *in* keeping. The one word that sounds like Richard.' Now what could have caused that sudden 'Hell! ' between the confession and the shot? Something absolutely soundless, otherwise we should hear it on the recording. Something that was annoying but which did not seem very serious to Richard, for it is his normal cheerful word of irritation. I maintain that there is only one possible thing. *The light went out.* The switch, as I noticed, in the bedside light was a lozenge switch in the cord which would make no sound at all. Someone, therefore, had come to Richard's room that evening, persuaded him to read a part in which the speaker confessed to the murder of a woman before committing suicide, persuaded him to let this be recorded, and having switched out the light, shot him through the head from below the chin, leaving the thing as a suicide. As simple as that.

" It would not, it seemed, be hard to make this convincing. In spite of his easy-going nature there was something about Richard which no one understood, and it is noteworthy that several of those who knew him best, including Keith and Pippa, told me that although they would not believe he had murdered anyone, they were quite prepared to think he had killed himself, in spite of his cheerful behaviour that day, testified to by Mr Toffin and Miss Hipps, and during the previous week, testified to by almost everyone.

" Someone phoned him at the shop after Mr Toffin had left that afternoon and had a long conversation with him. Miss Hipps, who was of a sentimentally jealous disposition, went in to interrupt it and heard Richard say " Ten o'clock then ", before hanging up. It seems safe to assume that this was the murderer. Soon afterwards Richard asked for the tape-recorder, which he later took up to his flat. He had nothing to do till the Beethoven Trio, which he wanted to hear, came on at 9.15, so he took his car out. He was perhaps about to visit his aunt at Drumbone House when he met Wilma Day and drove her to the station. What time he re-entered we do not know, for the only person who might have seen, Slugley the porter, can't or won't tell us. But it is not very important."

Carolus was interrupted by the headmaster.

" This is extremely interesting," he said, " and much of it carries conviction. But having made a cross-channel journey by air and slept ill, I am tempted to regale myself with another small drink. Inspector? Whisky. Deene? The same. Er Mrs. . . . Er Stout. You, Priggley, are doubtless enjoying a lemonade. Beer? Well, perhaps on this occasion. We have all felt our anxieties."

Bowler spoke sharply.

"I wish you'd come to the point, Mr Deene," he said.

The headmaster smiled and shook his head.

"I fear there is no hurrying him. I speak from some experience of Deene's methods, some of it like this unfortunate case of a very anxious and unhappy nature. I have found it useless to attempt to hasten his conclusions."

"Cheerio, sir," said Priggley, raising his glass.

"Er cheer-er-rio, Priggley," responded Mr Gorringer. "Yes, I shall not attempt to hurry you, Deene. At the same time there is a question which I cannot suppress. You have told us that Richard Hoysden was murdered and you have explained how this was done. But you have not yet suggested a motive. I confess I am baffled. What motive could there be for the murder of this very inoffensive man?"

"There could have been a good many," said Carolus. "There was in fact a very adequate one. Nobody could so convincingly carry the onus for the murder of a woman. Have you forgotten the rest of the recording? 'I strangled her'."

"You mean that the murderer, having committed the crime he intended, added yet another to his charge in order to provide a scapegoat who would distract all suspicion from him?"

"That was the idea, yes. Otherwise, why all that about having killed a woman? If someone merely wanted to kill Richard and make it look like suicide he would have been satisfied with the recording of a far simpler and more convincing suicide speech. If there was not another murder, in fact, the manner of Richard's death would be itself suspect. It was an ingenious idea, too, and nearly succeeded. Nobody really doubted when they heard that recording that Richard had killed a woman, in spite of their loyal assurances that it was impossible. If the whole thing had gone as it was planned no one would ever have doubted it. In that case, the woman would have been found before, or at the same time as, Richard; there would have been no suspicion at all, and I should never have heard the recording."

"Ingenious indeed! " said Mr Gorringer, his protuberant eyes wide open. "The man must be a fiend in human shape."

"He is a murderer," said Carolus calmly. "Just once or twice in a generation there is born a natural murderer, a murderer of vocation, and the startling thing is that he is virtually unrecognizable. He is not a schizophrenic—his mind is far from split, on the contrary he might be called single-minded. Sometimes he begins his career quite young, sometimes he waits till he is past middle age, but most often he achieves his masterpieces when he is in the prime of life. In this case we had such a murderer, one who simply was not interested in personal ties, or obligations, in natural human affections or loyalties, who was as cold-blooded as a fish in Arctic waters, cruel, ruthless and utterly resolute, and yet who had the faculty possessed by such murderers of appearing a normal, even an amiable person.

"That is what has made this interesting, in a macabre way. This was no impulsive killing, no crime of passion, not even a murder for greed, as it turned out. Here were the actions of someone whom the psychiatrists would call stark raving mad, and whom I consider to be that *rara avis* a murderer born, a murderer by natural talent, a murderer who would stop at nothing. It was particularly interesting because fate turned against this murderer and the whole thing lost all recognizable pattern.

"What was accomplished was accomplished with brilliance. All the details of Richard's ' suicide ' save that small exclamation ' Hell! ' went exactly according to plan. The murderer was not seen coming into the building, the tape-recorder had been brought up by Richard and worked perfectly, not a finger-print was left . . ."

"Don't be too sure of that," said Bowler, "we did not get the tape-recorder till it was too late to find any, but that was one place they must have been. Couldn't have wiped them off because it was going."

"True," said Carolus, "a good example of the danger of suppressing evidence. But the shot was at the right angle, the pistol in the right place, the light was left on and the curtains drawn close. Not an error. As for the rhetorical nature of the confession, that could have been got over at a long stretch. A suicide might, I suppose, have committed it to memory. 'Hell' was the only slip and its significance would not have been noticed if the rest of the plan had gone well."

"You mean," said Mr Gorringer pompously, "you mean all this was part of a plot to kill the game-keeper's wife, Florrie Lamplow?"

Carolus looked at him with sympathy.

"Oh, no," he said. "It was part of a plot to kill Lady Drumbone."

20

QUICKLY, before there could be ponderous exclamations of surprise or incredulity from Mr Gorringer, Carolus continued:

"The idea was this. Good-natured Richard Hoysden was to read his confession and die somewhere between ten and eleven, then between eleven and twelve the murderer was to go to Lady Drumbone's flat, of which everyone had keys, remember, and strangle her with the cord of the oyster-coloured curtains in the room called 'the lounge'. The whole of the confession had been most artfully written to meet the two contingencies. To Richard it would seem a piece of melodramatic rhetoric with no particular application; to anyone hearing it who knew that Lady Drumbone had been strangled with her own curtain-cord, it would be damaging and conclusive.

"Both of these people could be counted on to be alone, Richard because his wife had left him and his movements were familiar to everyone, Lady Drumbone because of the idyll planned by Keith and Wilma Day at Marling Flats. Neither would be discovered till the morning, by which time it would be quite impossible for anyone to say that they had, as it were, died in the wrong order. As you probably know, a great deal of nonsense has been talked about *rigor mortis* and the time of death, and one reads sometimes of a doctor giving one glance at a corpse and saying 'yes, died at 5.45 last Tuesday'. Many factors influence any conjecture—for it can scarcely be more than that—but certainly the most any doctor could have said in this case would have been that both had died between, say nine p.m. and one a.m., which was what the murderer wanted. You will not have failed to notice the green carpet at Lady Drumbone's—'white on the green ground'.

"When I had reached this point I was pretty sure of the murderer's identity, and I do not propose to go on talking ambiguously about him for long. It would be affectation to continue as though he might be a woman, for I doubt if any woman in this case would have the sheer physical strength to carry out the whole thing, and these were not women's crimes, anyway. But though Detective Inspector Bowler knows who it is, since he has him under arrest, and although the rest of you will know in a moment if you don't know already, long custom constrains me to hold back his name till the last moment.

"Richard safely dead, he proceeded to the second part of his plan, and it was now that he met his obstacle, for at Drumbone House Pippa had arrived. Pippa, Lady Drumbone and Keith sat talking in 'the lounge' and it was quite certain that Pippa was staying the night.

"The murderer was now faced with a dangerous predicament. There was the dead body of Richard, and it would only be thought to be suicide if his victim was discovered.

If Richard had not killed a woman it would be evident that he had not killed himself either, and before long there would be suspicion of murder culminating in the murderer's arrest.

"Fortunately for him, in wording the confession so ambiguously that Richard would notice nothing, the murderer had unwittingly given himself scope to deal with the present situation. With what relief he must have thought of Florrie Lamplow, alone in a lonely cottage at a convenient distance from the town yet far enough from her next-door neighbours to be beyond the range of their observation. There was the additional luck, of which he may or may not have been aware, that there had been, as Mrs Tuck had told me, some local talk about Richard and Florrie. If the murderer was aware of this it must have seemed to him to make his case cast-iron. Richard, anxious to return to his wife, had gone out and murdered Florrie then returned and killed himself in remorse. It was not the murder originally planned and it had not the original motive, but as a cover-up for any possible question over Richard's suicide it could not have been better.

"He was known to Florrie Lamplow, who came down to open the door to him. This was I think, as Mrs Redlove maintained, about two in the morning. He had taken Richard's car from the car park by which Slugley slept, and he was at the cottage for an unknown period since Mrs Redlove had 'dozed off' again before she heard him leave.

"He wanted the body to be discovered soon, but in a place likely to have been chosen by Richard. That is what I meant when I told Inspector Bowler that in looking in the places where Richard Hoysden would have left a body I was doing the commonsense thing. The murderer would have chosen one of those places, I argued. In fact he chose the clearing near the house, where we found it. He could not, unfortunately, leave the silk cord with the tassels like epaulettes on the dead shoulders, but at least he could use the designed method—strangulation and hope that the absence of the silk cord would not be noticed, or it would

184

be thought that this was raving on Richard's part or that someone had removed it.

"His scheme was nearly successful. It was true that he would have to wait some considerable time and work out something quite different in order to remove Lady Drumbone, his primary object. But he had recouped his losses very well. For his night's work he had left a strangled woman and a man who had shot himself having confessed to strangling her, and there was nothing in this that could involve him. He had the born murderer's gift of patience and was quite willing to wait for another occasion. That he *had* covered up well is shown by the fact that after the discovery of Florrie's body none of Richard's family, not even Lady Drumbone, doubted that Richard had killed her. I shall not easily forget Lady Drumbone's surprise when I told her he had not done so.

"So at this point, though I had my reasons for being pretty sure of the murderer's identity, I was faced with six—I won't say suspects, because it is too strong a word, but six persons who could be said to have some sort of motive, who had, at least so far as I knew for certain, the opportunity, and who had the means. In the case of each there was something pretty strong against believing him guilty, but while I had no absolute proof against my own suspect, I had to consider the case against each of these.

"To take the family first, there was Alan Bourne. He had the motive they all had—for remember we must look for motives for killing Lady Drumbone, no one else. He had told me that no one knew what Lady Drumbone had to leave, but it was obviously a great deal. He suffered from her autocracy as I noticed on the first evening when she offered drinks to me and deliberately did not invite her nephews, who dared not protest. He had access to the pistol and could drive out to Flogmore. He had learned from Pippa that she intended to stay the night at Lady Drumbone's and so could know that the second half of his plan was impossible. But against this, and to clear Alan, was first his wife's evidence, then the fact that these circum-

185

stances would have meant that he had killed Richard before he met Pippa. This is not quite impossible, but it discounts the evidence of Mrs Nodges and Mr Hoskins about the time of the shots.

"Then Keith. He had all the same motives as Alan and perhaps better opportunities, because he could wait until Pippa had finally gone to bed and then slip out. But against this was the fact that he had intended going to Wilma Day at the bungalow that night, and when I overheard their conversation I *knew* that he had intended to come and was deeply in love with her. Moreover there was his youth.

"Youth, too, was against suspecting Charles Bourne, though Slugley claimed to have seen him, or someone suspiciously like him, leaving the block of flats that night after coming from Richard's. Moreover, though one might conceivably convince oneself that he had some motive for killing Richard, it is hard to say why he should plot an elaborate double murder to kill Lady Drumbone.

"Slugley had the three essentials, motive (of a sort), means and opportunity. But unless Richard himself had taken the pistol from Alan's house it is hard to see how Slugley could have had it to use that evening. It is unlikely, too, that he knew of the family's visits to Flogmore or, if he did, of their favourite picnic spots.

"Toffin had everything as a suspect, except probability. I could not, somehow, bring myself to see him in the part. His enthusiasm for amateur theatricals and his knowledge that Richard might be inveigled into a part could account for his presence in Richard's flat and the tape-recording. It was the rest of the programme that seemed almost to rule him out.

"Finally there was Rothsay. He, again, had motive, opportunity and means. I admitted to myself that like Slugley he was either a stupid man or one clever enough to appear stupid. He *could* have known all about Flogmore woods, and certainly his car was in the car-park near Richard's flat that evening. But I did not fancy him as a suspect. His car could have been where Slugley saw it while he had a drink at the Fox and Hounds, as Slugley admitted, and if he had entered the block with the express purpose of killing Richard he would scarcely have left it there to be seen. Moreover, he had had no opportunity to get possession of the revolver with which Richard was killed.

"However, none of these five could be quite ruled out . . ."

Mr Gorringer raised his hand.

"Let us pause for a moment," he suggested, "and perhaps"—he looked enquiringly about him—"once more relieve our thirst."

Knowing that the round the headmaster had bought was already regarded by him as something of an extravagance, Carolus was about to order when Bowler spoke.

"I think in view of your elaborate theorizing, Mr Deene, we might run to one out of Expenses." He pushed the bell.

"Well," remarked Mrs Tuck, "I never thought I'd get a drink from a copper. Nor accept it, either. But since They're paying for it, cheerio."

Mr Gorringer's good humour was returning to him and he no longer seemed so anxiously concerned about the reputation of his school.

"There is a piece of evidence, related to me by Priggley," he announced, "which strikes me as particularly telling. One of the tenants of flats above Richard Hoysden's, a Mrs Nodges, believed she heard the sound of a shot at the mysterious hour of 4 a.m. What of that?"

Carolus grinned.

"As I tackle more problems," he said, "I find the necessity increases of distinguishing between evidence and what I may call natural red herrings. This was one of these. The woman believed she heard something, but as her husband told her, her mind was full of shots. This time it may really have been a car backfiring. At all events, so far as I can see, it had nothing to do with the case. Certainly no second shot was fired in Richard's flat."

Mr Gorringer cleared his throat.

"As something of an *aficionado* in these matters," he said, "forced into association with them by Deene's predilections, I cannot but admire the way he has drawn us off the scent, as it were. It is quite evident that the murderer was not among the five persons mentioned."

"Who was it then?" asked Carolus, somewhat surprised.

Mr Gorringer allowed an expression of great cunning to overspread his face.

"Come now, Deene. It is all too obvious. It was the tenant of the flat above Hoysden's who claimed to have heard a shot. Hoskins, I mean."

"But why, headmaster? On what do you base that?"

"Aha," said Mr Gorringer, "old birds are not to be caught with chaff. I sensed it as soon as you failed to name him among your 'possibles'."

"In other words you simply guessed the least likely person and gambled on it. No, I said right at the beginning of this case that it was one in which not to be afraid of the obvious. The murderer was, of course, Keith Bourne.

"In considering him just now I said that what seemed to clear him was his appointment with Wilma Day at Marling Flats. But if we examine that a moment we shall see that it is precisely what incriminates him. For the original plot an alibi was necessary and Wilma was to provide this. In that conversation I overheard were these significant words. 'Had you given up hope by then?' asked Keith. 'Darling, don't be absurd. I'd *no* idea what time it was till it started getting light. You knew I hadn't a watch. You were taking it to . . .' Keith in other words, on a pretext of having Wilma's watch adjusted, repaired or cleaned, made sure that she would not know the time when he arrived at the bungalow. He would perhaps hand her her watch set back an hour or so, to match his own. So that if he had finished what he had to do in Maresfield by eleven-thirty as he hoped, and reached the bungalow within an hour of that, he would have someone to swear he had been there since eleven, an excellent alibi.

"Apart from that all the probabilities were with him.

He was the only one who had a real and urgent motive for murdering Lady Drumbone, and if you're going to tell me that to a pathological murderer of twenty-one the ambition to marry a girl and start a repertory theatre does not constitute a motive, I shall say that the facts confute you. He had worked out every detail of his theatre, found the place for it and knew the capital needed. For both of these things he needed only the money he would inherit from his aunt. His lies to me about that were highly indicative. He did not know how his aunt felt about him and Wilma. 'We've never let her guess,' he said. He did not see why he should anticipate opposition to the repertory theatre from his aunt. 'It's just that I haven't had the guts to tell her yet.' He knew perfectly well that his aunt, as she told me, had flatly refused to countenance either of his projects, but he did not mean to let me guess that he had a motive for killing her.

"Yes, he planned very efficiently. His first idea was that Richard should appear to have shot himself with Tom Lamplow's Savage 30·30 rifle, and went out with his sister to get hold of it. This was easy, as it happened, because the two women left him and went upstairs because Florrie had a present for Olivia. 'All very mysterious'. Olivia recalled Florrie saying 'Come up to my room because I've got something for you'. Keith wasn't even allowed to see it. But while they were upstairs he had plenty of time to put the rifle in his car.

"However, that afternoon at Anita's tennis party, a better idea occurred to him—the revolver and ammunition which Alan kept so carelessly locked up in his room. This was better because it would avoid the difficulty of getting the rifle into Richard's flat—cricket-bag or golf clubs or whatnot—and it would look as though Richard himself had taken it that afternoon. Keith even went so far as to say to me when I asked him if Richard could have taken the revolver—'I suppose so, yes. I believe he stayed upstairs for a shower when we went down for drinks.'

"So he rang Richard up at the shop and told him about

the play he was writing. As Pippa had told me, 'Keith I didn't mind so much, though he was always coming to Richard for advice or with schemes for something he wanted to write'. There was nothing unusual in this then. Would Richard bring up a tape-recorder because it would be wonderful to try it out and Richard could read so well and so on. (To me he flatly denied 'writing'. Any of the other arts, but 'that at least I know I can't do'.) Richard did, and as he finished that very artfully written confession Keith, who was sitting beside the bed, silently switched off the light. 'Hell! ' said Richard, and it was his last word. With extraordinary *sang froid* Keith shot him from under the chin through the head. He switched on the light again, letting Richard fall into a natural position, wiped his own finger-prints from the revolver and put it in Richard's hand for *his*, then put it on the floor. Everything he did in complete silence because all the time the tape-recorder was running.

"He had prepared for his leaving the house. He had noticed yesterday that Charles's arm was in a sling and had brought one in his pocket. He slipped it on, also a Grammar School cap and a pair of sun-glasses. He was much the same size as Charles and he looked so young in face that I was able to convince my housekeeper that he was a friend of Priggley's. But he wore these only to the public lavatory at the corner, I guess. I remember almost hoping that Charles would say he had been to the flat that evening. for I did not suspect him, and this would have exonerated Keith. I told him that everything depends on his word about this. But of course he had not been there and there was only one person young enough to dare wear a schoolboy's cap even for that short distance and at night, and that was Keith. I was interested to notice how Keith probed in questions to me to find out if I knew of that 'schoolboy's' departure. 'I suppose someone could have gone to the flat without Slugley noticing', and so on.

"But when he reached Drumbone House he found that Pippa had arrived unexpectedly at 11.5 and was staying the night. It meant that the rest of his scheme was off. You may remember that he was 'flabbergasted' to see her. I would like to know how quickly he realized his position. He had, as it were, 'wasted' one perfectly executed murder and would have to carry out another, equally futile, to save himself from any possible suspicion.

"He took Richard's car, as Slugley heard, at about two o'clock. He was not going to take the chance of driving his own noticeable sports car. If a car was to be noticed it must be Richard's. After all, the timing might stretch wide enough for Richard to have murdered Florrie at this time and shot himself afterwards. But he was not seen. All Mrs Redlove could say was that it sounded like an 'ordinary' car.

"His only anxiety after that was that Florrie's body should be found. Until then the circumstances of Richard's death were curious and his 'confession' unaccountable. But he was too clever to lead anyone to it, by either word or action. How brilliantly and naturally he consented to lead me through Flogmore woods, saying that of course we should find nothing. He started at the wrong end of Tom's beat and worked back to the beginning, allowing Priggley to exclaim on seeing the corpse which Keith knew was there. He was aided by nature then, for he naturally felt sick, but it was all beautifully misleading.

"I still had no proof. There was no one else who could have done it, in my eyes, but that doesn't constitute proof. I had to work something out.

"Perhaps what I did was somewhat elaborate, but it worked. I gambled on one thing—that he didn't know I knew about the gun. It was extremely unlikely, after all. Florrie had had only one day in which to notice its disappearance and was notoriously reticent with her neighbours. She *had* noticed it and, what is more, I believe, suspected Keith of taking it. 'The thought of who might have it', worried her more than its disappearance, according to Mrs Beale.

"I don't know how he explained to himself the fact that

I was to stay at the game-keeper's cottage. He suspected a trap, but luck had been with him, and like most paranoiacs he underrated his opponents. He came out determined to kill me, as I knew he would, but with the safeguard that if he was seen or caught he was coming to my assistance. Hadn't he been heard asking if he might accompany me? When he had killed me he would rouse the district to say that he had found me dead. It was a fairly safe bet. A schoolmaster alone in a lonely cottage at night would be no match for a now hardened murderer with a Savage 30·30 rifle.

"You know the rest. The noticeable suit, the lamplight and the open book—it was an easy shot and he did not hesitate. Then that 'megaphone-microphone-magnified' voice above him in the trees—he did as I hoped he would, dropped the rifle and made for his car. My only fear was that he would hang on to the rifle, but there wasn't much danger of that, really. It's a primitive instinct to drop anything heavy before running, and he obeyed it. I had the car ready if he hadn't, but I was fairly confident. So, after all, it was a case for finger-prints. There's a tendency to belittle their importance in detection nowadays, but never by me.

"And knowing something of the pathological murderer, the murderer born, I should not be surprised if he has already made a long and boastful statement, admitting, or rather glorying in everything. Am I right, Inspector?"

Bowler hesitated, seeming to consider whether an answer would be a breach of professional etiquette. Then as they all watched him he slowly nodded his head.